DEEP ELLUM

*

BY

BRANDON HOBSON

DEEP ELLUM

ISBN: 978-1-940853-01-7

cover & design by Cal A. Mari

Excerpts from *Deep Ellum* appeared, sometimes in radically different form, in *NOON*, *Web Conjunctions* and *The Literarian*.

published by Calamari Press
NY, NY

< www.calamaripress.com >

For Ian and Holden

Walked up Ellum and I come down Main
Tryin' to bum a nickle, just to buy cocaine
—Lead Belly

I left Chicago and returned to Dallas when our mother overdosed. She'd tried it before, usually with pills, but this time they hospitalized her and put her on different medication. Before, whenever she wasn't taking her meds, my stepfather Gene would find her wading in Skeleton Creek or harassing old man Skinner at the bait-and-tackle shop down the road from where they lived in the country. I was worried about her more this time, even though we'd been through it before.

I took a taxi from the airport to my sister's place near downtown Dallas, in the Deep Ellum district, past the old buildings and neighborhoods with cars parked in yards, wood-framed houses with chipped paint. I was twenty-six. The city felt foreign to me even though I hadn't been away that long. I told the driver to take his time driving.

"I don't understand," he said.

My last night in Chicago my friend Santiago took me to a bar where I met a woman who told me that the lack of excess and chance is the beginning of failure. Don't go home, she said. Don't fly to a damp wasteland, emptiness, fields. There's nothing down there anymore.

"I mean there's no hurry," I told the driver.

To pursue solitude requires a sort of minimal desire, or maybe no desire at all. This is how I see it. To find loneliness, to become your own saint. To desire solitude and be with my mother until I felt safe enough to leave again. In Chicago I lived in an apartment with four other people. I waited tables at a restaurant and worked a few days a week in a cafeteria. When my sister Meg called and told me about our mother's suicide attempt, I had to leave.

I was in Chicago almost a year. My girlfriend's job transferred her there, so I went along. Six months later we weren't getting along and she wanted me out of the apartment. So I got a job waiting tables at a restaurant and moved in with a couple of guys I worked with. I'd never gone to college and had worked shit jobs mostly, roofing and painting houses and waiting tables. My brother Basille said I was always running away, but there was nothing to run away from.

I went to the apartment on Deep Ellum Alley, a room overlooking warehouses and buildings and the dirty street below. Meg had given me a key after she'd moved in over a year ago. The room was cold and dark. I was surprised the place was neat and clean, not filled with articles of clothing draped over chairs or all over the floor as I had expected. Her bed was made; it seemed she'd been away for a couple of days. There was a bird in a cage, a gray and yellow cockatiel. It fluttered its wings, cocked its head and looked at me. I put my bag down and opened the refrigerator. There was orange juice and bread, a six-pack of schwag beer. Meg had terrible taste in beer. No coffee. On the window ledge there was a patch of old snow, ash-light breaking in.

I needed to go out for cigarettes. I found one of Meg's coats in the closet and put it on over my hooded sweatshirt. Before I left Chicago I'd given my coat to a kid wearing a Bears T-shirt. He was handing out copies of his own music. "Psychedelic funk," he told me. "You'll like it." I traded him the coat for one of his CDs. "Where you from?" he asked.

"Dallas."

"Me too," he said.

Meg's coat fit me OK. I stopped to look at myself in her bathroom mirror. A bottom tooth near the back was sore. I opened my mouth, not knowing what I was looking for. There was a sharp pain in the gum—a cavity maybe, or something else. I looked through the medicine cabinet and found bottles of aspirin and Ibuprofen, heartburn tablets, allergy capsules, lotions, tubes, gels. I took four Ibuprofen and headed out.

As evening fell, Crowdus Street was dark and a light snow was falling. Buildings looked small and crooked, deprived of sunlight. Structures in Chicago were proportioned and near exact—buildings of art. Here, there was no color anywhere. A grainy film, something out of an old photograph. A man in a long coat and a

Dallas Cowboys stocking cap leaned forward and coughed, on the verge of sickness. Only his right hand was gloved. A few blocks away I found a 7-11. Behind the counter, the clerk was talking in Spanish on his cell phone and trying to write something down. An older couple with a miniature bull terrier on a leash was arguing about something. The woman looked at me as I knelt down to scratch the dog behind the ear. I bought a pack of Camels and left.

The last time I was in Deep Ellum there were people all around, but the weather was better then. I made my way down the block, down Malcolm X Boulevard in the cold wind—the same block I had walked down a year earlier, before I left for Chicago. I could imagine myself walking like this for a long time. All around me was narrowness and shadows, brick buildings, the street. The air was heavy and dead. This was the function of Middle America cities in winter—rank smells, empty streets, narrow alleys and shadows. A woman standing in front of a sushi restaurant told me where the closest liquor store was. It wasn't too far, a few blocks away. I crossed Main and walked down a dark street. The guy working the liquor store had a cat with him. The cat was silent, slinking around my legs. A man watching me whispered something to the woman with him. I picked up the cat and let it curl against my chest. The couple watched me but I ignored them. I bought a bottle of vodka and headed back to Meg's place.

She still wasn't there. I unpacked in the bedroom, checked my cell phone, looked in all the dressers for pain pills, maybe some pot or even Ecstasy to chew up. I checked all the kitchen cabinets but found nothing. It was dark out. January, dead winter. I sat on the bed and watched a light snow. In the dim light of the streetlamps, the snow sifted down. In Chicago I could sit at the window forever and watch the snow.

I tried to call our mother's house. Two weeks earlier Meg had called and told me our mother had quit taking her meds. She was severely depressed, immobile, staying in bed all the time. Our stepfather Gene rarely returned my calls. We never got along, not even when I was a kid. He worked his whole life in a foundry, where he dragged giant buckets of hot white metal across an overhead track and poured the buckets into molds. Our mother told him he was lucky to be alive, breathing in all that aluminum and iron and asbestos. At some point he'd developed the shakes. Looking at him you'd think he was a meth-head, the way he twitched around all the time. For a while, just before I left for Chicago, my ex-girlfriend and I lived six blocks from the factory where he worked, past the railyard, in the run-down, older district near downtown.

I called our mother's house and left a message: "It's Gideon, I'm back in Dallas. I'm at Meg's. I hope you're feeling better. Give me a call."

In the kitchen I toasted some bagels. I ate standing, listening to the sound of pipes knocking. The sink was half full of used water. Everyone handles loneliness different. I didn't handle things well. That's what Meg always said. I opened the vodka and poured a glass, then sat at the window and watched the snow until I started feeling drunk. My tooth and gum were still sore and I was freezing. I put on Meg's coat and fell asleep in a chair.

-2-

In sleep I was passing crowds of people in a train station, looking for someone to help me find the train I was supposed to be on. A tall Asian girl in pigtails was staring at me. She was naked, wearing only black boots, but nobody noticed her except me. She was laughing. When I tried to move closer to her I kept getting lost in the shuffle of people. Someone pulled on my shirt but I didn't bother turning around. The Asian girl was there and then she wasn't.

I woke to someone knocking on the door. Through the peephole I saw a guy in a hoodie blowing in his hands. With the chain locked I cracked the door just enough to peek out. He looked surprised to see me.

"Oh hey," he said. "I was looking for Meg."

"My sister?"

"Is she here?"

"Sorry. I haven't seen her yet."

He blew on his hands. Pulled the hood down of his sweatshirt, revealing a tangle of long hair. I looked past him to see if he was alone.

"I'm Charlie," he said. "A friend of Meg's. Can I come in for a second?"

"Okay," I said. "But just you." I unlocked the chain and let him in. He held out his hand for me to shake. He was older than me and had a scab on his bottom lip. It was cherry-dark and looked sore.

"Meg mentioned you," he said. "She said you were sick or something?"

"Sick?"

"You were depressed and living somewhere."

"Maybe she meant our mom."

9

"Right," he said, looking around the room. "Do you care if I make coffee?"

I sat in the chair by the window. Outside it was morning, cloudy and cold, snow on the ground. There were noises from the street, men unloading a truck. Charlie asked if I wanted any. I told him no.

"Funny thing," he said. "Meg always hides her coffee under the sink. She thinks nobody can find it. She told me a story about you once, how you got caught stealing a jar of sweet relish from the grocery store. You were a kid. You told the store manager to go fuck himself."

"That was our brother, Basille."

"Right," he said. "The one with the birthmark."

I turned and looked at him, then back out the window. Basille didn't have a birthmark. Charlie was opening and closing cabinets and drawers, and I worried he was up to something. Dishes and pans rattled as he rummaged. He said something about being in west Texas, but I zoned out and thought about my mother. I hoped she would call soon.

"Meg wasn't here last night?" Charlie asked.

"No."

"All right. You care if I use the bathroom?"

"Go ahead."

I heard him shut the door and turn on the faucet. He wasn't in there long. He came back into the kitchen and poured a cup of coffee. He sat across from me and we both looked out the window. After a moment he was standing again. "Can you tell Meg to call me when she gets here," he said. "She won't mind if I borrow this mug, OK? That girl—probably somewhere shooting something between her toes. Thanks for the coffee, brother."

He left, closing the door behind him. I stayed in the chair and looked out the window until I saw him emerge below onto the street. He put his hood up and crossed Crowdus. There was someone else across the street. He stopped and talked to the guy and they walked away together.

Meg's things were everywhere in the bedroom. Unorganized clutter, objects of her past life, things without value—catalogues, magazines, postcards, nail polish, guitar picks, CDs, a pair of sunglasses, a deck of Las Vegas Club cards, envelopes, ballpoint pens and loose pages of sheet music. I took some postcards from the dresser and decided to write the people I missed in Chicago. The postcards had pictures of beaches and well-lit buildings at night from places like Los Angeles, San Diego, Las Vegas. I wrote my name on each one. Addressed them to Marc Kolliopoulos, Lucy Kern and the Chicago bands I liked: Spit, Los Olvidados. The jazz musicians Moses James and Doc Robinson.

"Tell the derelicts hello," I wrote. I drew pictures of trumpets and ears. It was important to keep contact with them since I wanted to return there at some point.

My tooth was hurting. I went out for food and to mail the postcards. On the way out, sitting on the stairs was a girl in her late twenties, maybe early thirties. She was doing something with her cell phone. She looked up at me as I came out of the apartment.

"Hey," she said. "Are you Gideon? Meg's brother."

She was wearing a black leather jacket and a scarf around her neck, her hair in a ponytail. She was sitting on the top step, leaning against the rail. She resembled the girl in Chicago who told me not to leave. There's nothing for you down there, the girl had said.

"Who are you?" I asked.

"Desi," she said. "Not Desiree. Just Desi. Nice coat. I saw you walking outside the building yesterday with your bag over your shoulder."

"I just got here last night."

"You OK? You look sort of tired. Don't take that the wrong way, just saying is all. I live downstairs, right below you. Below

Meg. I hear her footsteps all the time. I heard yours earlier, a little while ago when I was watching my cat play."

I found myself staring at her mouth. It reminded me of someone. "Have you seen Meg?" I asked.

"I was about to ask you the same. She might be staying with Axel. Or maybe she's with Kim and Danielle. She's around somewhere. Did she know you were coming?"

"She knows. We talked last week."

"Maybe she's out giving an oath in blood. Buying some nothing dope. Right? I'm sure she's around somewhere."

"I have to go mail these," I said, showing her the postcards.

"Just Desi," she said. "Not Desiree. You got it?"

"Maybe you're a lead singer in a band or something."

She was digging in her purse. "No, but I keep an open mind. You want I can make you something to eat sometime? I have fresh asparagus from the country. Cool?"

Outside, the wind was cold and blowing. Papers flew around. I buttoned Meg's coat and headed south. Down Malcolm X Boulevard a few blocks, a man in a black coat was waiting at the bus stop. He kept lifting a finger and pointing at something in the sky, as if aiming. He wore a fedora and had a gray beard. I stopped at the corner and waited to cross. A woman standing next to me was talking to someone on her cell. She kept saying, "He's sick, Burt. It's his problem. The whole thing's sick."

Another block away I found a mailbox and dropped the postcards into it. There was a burger place down the street. I got a cheeseburger and fries to go and headed back to the apartment. A preacher was on the side of a road, shouting something about freedom and spirits. He was wearing an old coat and dirty jeans. He looked to be in his forties or fifties, and nobody was paying any attention to him. I could see the pain in his face, the suffering, the sadness. This man, standing outside in the cold wind and snow, calling out a message to nobody. In Chicago I'd seen people walking down the street, mumbling to themselves. I realized I was doing this now.

When I got back to the apartment, my friend Sawyer Cline was waiting upstairs at the door. I hadn't seen Sawyer since before I left for Chicago. He was living with a couple of guys he worked with. They had Monday Night Football parties and people staying over all the time. Sawyer was dyspneic and overweight. He liked to smoke hydroponic pot while listening to Jane's Addiction and eating Nutter Butters. When he was seventeen he got drunk and stole a car from the neighborhood, put it through the window of Repo Records and then got out and asked if they had anything by Throbbing Gristle. "But all that is history," he always said.

Sawyer had lost a little weight, which was the first thing I told him when I saw him at Meg's apartment.

"I'm still fat," he told me. "Hey, I sent you like thirty texts last night and never heard back. Thought maybe your plane crashed or something. I was worried they'd have to fish your body parts out of a ditch or some shit." He came over and hugged me. He was always hugging people. We went inside and sat on the floor so I could eat.

When we were in our teens Sawyer and I would sometimes skip class and drive around and get high. He drove his mother's beat-up Crown Vic since he didn't have his own car, and I didn't have one either. He'd come and pick me up for school and we'd drive around by the lake where there was no traffic, listening to a CD of Sawyer reading his own autobiography that he was in the process of writing in third person. He claimed he was a quarter Cherokee Indian and had ancestors who walked the Trail of Tears, which was entirely false.

Sawyer was always a terrible liar. The most pathetic lie I ever heard him tell was to his parents when we were seventeen and they returned home after being gone for a weekend. Sawyer was instructed not to drive his mother's Crown Vic while they were out of town, but on Saturday night he drove it over to my house, picked me up and we went over to our friend Colin's to hang out and drink. On the way back we pulled into the parking lot at KFC and Sawyer hit a dumpster, denting the front fender. I was standing there when his parents came home and Sawyer reeled off a story about how some teenage gang members had shown up from south Dallas and threatened to shoot us if he didn't give them the keys to the car, and that those guys took the car for a 30-45 minute joyride and then returned it. When Sawyer's mother asked why we didn't call the police he told her the gang members tied us with rope back-to-back in the dining room chairs and threatened to come back and stab us if we told anyone. Sawyer said we finally managed to wriggle ourselves out of the knotted ropes later that night. His father was beyond livid.

"Rope?" he'd said. "Where's the goddamn rope, Sawyer?"

You could see the spittle on Mr. Cline's lips as he yelled, hyperventilating.

These days Sawyer seemed different. In Meg's apartment, he acted distracted, almost unhappy.

"How's your band?" I asked.

"Forehead Orgy split up two months ago. Couldn't get many gigs as a polka band. We played a couple of weddings, but they made us change our name. Then Cale freaked out and quit and joined a Smiths tribute band."

"You working?"

"I'm still at Taco Hut, if that's what you mean. Don't think I'm a loser, though. It's temporary. The place doesn't smell of two-day old hooker crotch anymore. I'm still thinking about culinary school. How's your mom? You talk to her yet?"

"Called her last night. I'm going out to see her when Meg gets in."

I took my cell out of the coat pocket and saw Sawyer's texts, but I didn't have any voice messages. I sent Meg another text: *Where r u? I'm here! At your apt.*

Sawyer had a joint in his coat pocket. When I finished eating we lit it and passed it back and forth. He held the joint to his lips with his thumb and index finger. We smoked it all the way down to the resin. Sawyer laughed in a cloud of smoke. I took off my shirt and laid back on the floor, hands behind my head, stretching out my legs. The ceiling was egg white with water stains. We were silent for a while, listening to the sounds the cockatiel made from its cage. The bird hopped from the perch and pecked at seeds, watching us as it ate.

"That bird," Sawyer said. "Weird."

Outside there was street noise. A bus droned by. Sawyer sat in the middle of the room, away from all corners. "Corners make me nervous," he said. "To be cornered in, trapped, backed against a wall. I need space."

14

I backed away to give him room to breathe. We didn't talk for what felt like a long time. Sawyer's eyes were closed. "You don't seem happy," he said.

"I was in Chicago, what do you expect? Now I'm back here."

He opened his eyes to slits. "I'm craving Arwal. You have one?"

"What?"

"Arwal," he said. "Meg usually has some. Really good shit, high street value. Hardly any side effects, mainly just a rash and sores on the lip. But worth it."

"Is it a pain killer? If so, I could use one."

"It's a pain killer, a hallucinogenic, a glimpse of heaven. For me, a dietary supplement. Other side-effects are that you hallucinate and see narwhals."

"Narwhals? The fish?"

"They're not fish, they're mammals. They're usually hiding behind dumpsters or in dark places."

"Mammals," I said, still lying on my back, staring up at the ceiling. The bird was making noise in its cage. Sawyer went through his coat pockets, looking for Arwal.

"Narwhals," I kept saying.

"I wonder if Meg has some around," he said. "You know where she keeps her weed and shit?"

"I couldn't find anything. But go ahead and look."

He went into Meg's bathroom and stayed for a while. When I went to check on him, I found him with his arm in the toilet. "Dropped my phone," he said. He fished it out and stared at it, dripping water. "What time is it?"

My phone showed 4:11.

"Shit, I have to be at work at four," he said. "I'll catch up with you later."

After he left I took off all my clothes and got into Meg's bed and fell asleep. I'm not sure how long I slept, but when I woke it was dark outside again.

-4-

It rained most of the night. I drank some vodka and went to the movies. Something French, with subtitles. The theatre was empty except for an older couple and some guy who sat in the back with his feet up. The film was black-and-white and the characters smoked cigarettes and talked in long, serious conversations. I couldn't follow the storyline. When I came out of the theatre I checked my cell, but nobody had called. The lobby was quiet and dim and smelled of popcorn. Outside it was still raining and cold. I pulled on my stocking cap and walked down the street to the bus stop. There wasn't anyone else around. The street felt empty and dark and dead.

Later I had another visitor. This time it was an older man who introduced himself as Warren Puig—a friend of Meg's who lived in a loft over on Commerce. He had disheveled white hair and a beard that covered most of his face. He wore baggy khaki pants and a ratty coat frayed at the cuffs. "I'm having a party this weekend," he told me. "Is Meg around?"

"Not yet," I said. "I'm her brother."

"Fantastic. The party is Friday at my place. I live with my girlfriend Sophia a few blocks away. I'm an artist. Actually, retired. I was a commercial artist for thirty years, but that's all history. What's your name?"

"Gideon."

"Fantastic," he said. He let himself in and walked over to the birdcage. He pointed his index finger into the cage so that the bird nibbled at it. "Don't worry about the party. I'm a normal guy. I put on my pants one leg at a time. My girlfriend is thirty-three years younger than me. She's complex, a piece of abstract art." He looked at me. "You single?"

"Yeah."

16

"Terrific. There'll be single people there, a variety of interesting people. Some failed at pornography in the eighties. Others are office drones, financial analysts. Maybe some musicians. I'll be the oldest, pushing sixty, so I won't dance. You ever seen an old guy dance? It's awkward and embarrassing for everyone. I hope you'll come with Meg. Where is she, by the way?"

"I haven't seen her. Just got in from Chicago last night."

I liked something about Puig, something genuine and fatherly. He appeared happy, talkative, the type of guy who'd trust you to housesit or drive his expensive car.

"Fantastic city," he said. "I played tennis there one summer with a man named Monolito from the Dominican Republic. This was years ago. I was there for a job interview. We smoked hashish with two twinks in a dirty apartment. Did yoga in the park. Somehow the gods aligned the weather for three days in a row of beautiful sunshine. This cold snap we're having is certainly no fun. The weather's extreme here, isn't it? Everywhere, really. It's not supposed to be this way."

He scratched his beard and looked up at the ceiling.

I needed to be alone. I wanted to go for a walk, roam around outside in the fresh air. I put on Meg's coat and told him I was sorry to rush off but that I had an appointment at the podiatrist for my foot.

"I can tell right away you walk with a slight limp. Your posture is interesting, not unlike Meg's. No sweat though, give my love to Meg. Hope to see you Friday."

After he left I went for a walk. I always liked to take walks by myself. There was a time when I felt attached to everything I saw in the world. As a kid I would sit for hours at my mother's house in the country, staring at trees. I would lie down in the grass and stare up at the sky in the summer. I caught myself fainting from the lyrics of certain songs. Falling over at the sight of a sun setting in a western sky. Kneeling down to play with an insect. Rolling around on a freshly mown lawn. Sitting childlike at the window and looking at birds.

A few blocks away I stood in front of the window of an antique store. Its windows were full of snow globes, Texas souvenirs, artifacts, rows of small objects. I bought a Christmas snow globe for my mother even though it was January. All Christmas merchandise was on sale for 50% off. Inside the snow globe was a Christmas tree. When I shook it, snow swirled around.

In the store I got a text from Meg: *Hey! You're here early? Didn't realize, so sorry! I'll be home tomorrow. Make yourself at home. xo Meg.*

I texted back: *Where r u? I'm worried.*

Meg: *I'm fine! At a friend's, but I'll be there tomorrow. C u then.*

When I came out of the store I saw Desi across the street, talking to an older man wearing a long coat. I lit a cigarette and watched them. She was laughing, they embraced and then the man walked off. She saw me and waved me over.

"Hey creepo," she said. "You following me? What's in the bag?"

"Snow globe. For my mother. Who's the guy?"

"My uncle who lives in a loft over on Second. Where you headed?"

"For a walk. I don't know."

"You want a coffee?"

We walked to a diner on Elm and sat in a booth. I hadn't really noticed until now how good-looking she was. Her hair was pulled back, her face well-proportioned, cheekbones prominent and skin near perfect. She wore a bandanna. There was a sort of gritty high fashion about her. A wool scarf looped twice around her neck and draped over one shoulder. She looked like the type of person who didn't take the world too seriously. We ordered coffee and she tried to smile, drawing her coat close around her.

"I didn't go to work today," she said. "I really didn't have much to do anyway."

"What do you do?"

"I'm a counselor at a juvenile detention center."

"Kids who are locked up?"

"Right. Sometimes the court places them in the custody of social services and they sit in detention and wait to be placed in group homes. Then they run away from the group homes and return to the streets, and the whole cycle starts over again." The juveniles she talked to during intakes—after they changed out of their street clothes and showered and put all their money and jewelry in baggies, after they carried their bed sheets and pillows down the hall to their rooms—they told her what happens when they return to the streets. "They always want to talk their first night," she said. "Especially the newcomers. Part of my job is just listening to them."

I could see the passion in her face. I thought: how great to love your job. She told me about C.J., a sixteen year old from the south side of Dallas. He'd lived in six different foster homes since he was twelve. His father was in a gang, doing time for possession of firearms and drug trafficking. "That's serious shit," I said.

We talked for a long time about troubled kids, school, those sorts of things. I told her about my friends living in Chicago. About one of my roommates, a struggling artist who built small structures out of broken glass and old knives and spoons. Desi told me she'd graduated with a degree in sociology from the University of Texas. Her job at Social Services was her first real job. I could tell she came from a family with money. She worked just to keep herself busy, she didn't need to. She went to private schools only to be a social worker. I couldn't understand it.

Then I told her that Meg had texted me. "She's coming soon," I said.

"She's staying with that guy Axel, right? Are you worried about her?"

"Should I be? I don't know Axel."

"She talks about him some. She talks about you a lot. I know more than you probably want me to know."

Sitting at the table next to us was a man wearing a military jacket with copper medals, bead necklaces and sunglasses. The girl sitting across from him—maybe it was his daughter—was playing with her cell phone.

"I met Warren Puig," I told her.

She laughed. "He's an art dealer or something? Dates someone like my age. He's harmless, though."

"He's having a party tomorrow night at his loft."

"He has a party about every other week. Don't expect much. So have you decided what you'll do now?"

"Maybe I'll go back to Meg's and take a nap."

"I meant with your life."

"Oh," I said. "I don't know. My brother's supposed to get me a job at a guitar shop his friend owns. Something temporary. I'd like to go back to Chicago soon. I don't know. I see people driving in rush hour and they're trying to get home to their wives or kids or whatever. But they're sitting in traffic and it's five-thirty and dark outside and cold, dead winter. And by the time they get home and change clothes and basically wind down they get to see their families for about two hours before their kids are going to bed. People do this."

"Maybe it's not so bad. Maybe these people love what they do and love their families. Maybe they consider themselves fortunate that they even have children or a spouse."

She had an elitist air about her. It had the force of something that made her appear intelligent and frail but ready to address her spectral pleasures. We left the diner and headed back to the apartment in a light rain. Desi sheltered me with a large pink umbrella as we headed north on Good Latimer. When we got to the building she thanked me for the coffee and asked if I wanted to meet her cat.

"Maybe later," I said. "I'm freezing right now and I need to nurse this tooth."

"Cavity?"

"I don't know. It's killing me."

"Your jaw's a little swollen. You should see a dentist."

I went upstairs and ran a hot bath. Meg had one of those little TV/radios on the counter in her bathroom. She always spent a lot of time in the bath, listening to music or reading. I turned on a local news channel and then got undressed and into the tub. On the TV, the news anchor was interviewing an older couple in south Dallas who were prophesying the end of the world. The man had a gray beard and wore a dirty suit. He lifted his arms, convulsing on the screen. His wife's lips were moving. "It's the end," the man kept saying.

5

Deep Ellum Alley was empty most of the night. On Crowdus, a group of boys huddled together beside a wall, then walked away. Around nine, Gene called from the hospital to tell me our mother was doing fine but didn't want to talk on the phone.

"She's tired," he said. "She's tired and doesn't feel well. They're letting us go home tomorrow. You're back in town?"

"I'm at Meg's. We'll head that way tomorrow I hope."

"Your mother will be glad to see you. She wants us all to spend time together. Right now I'm driving over to Frank and Juanita's so she can rest. I'm sitting here in the car looking at the city lights of Dallas. It's exhausting, all of it. When you're around it so much it starts to get to you. Maybe you understand, maybe you don't."

"Who's there with her?"

"Basille's staying the night. I needed a break."

When I was a kid, Basille and I spent afternoons drinking Gene's liquor and jumping on an old mattress in our backyard. At first I was jealous of Gene and all the time he spent with our mother. One day when they were first dating, our mother told me to get out of the house for a while because some people were coming over, so I went for a walk down to the creek. I smoked a cigarette and walked over to the supermarket, where an old woman looked at me and said: "You, young man, don't make good decisions." I recognized her. She worked at the pawnshop where we bought a toy trumpet for Basille. Our mother called Basille a great jazz trumpet player. We listened to music every night at home, especially when Gene was over. At the supermarket, I bought a soda and some gum. I walked home in the rain.

That day there was a party going on at our house. Some of the motorcycle men were there. They were always happy to see me. They hung around the bar where our mother worked. I looked for her but couldn't find her. Out back, Gene sat on the porch with a woman, drinking wine.

"What's going on?" I asked.

"Woof woof," he said.

They laughed and the woman handed me a cup. We drank wine and listened to music coming from inside. We could hear the tribe of kids in the yard next door. The rain stopped, but it was getting dark outside. Soon I was drunk.

"How old are you?" the woman asked me.

"Twelve."

She looked at Gene and they laughed. I don't know why they kept laughing at me. I've thought about it over the years. I went back inside where loud music was playing. Basille was somehow asleep in his room. In the hall bathroom, our mother was laughing at a man who was kissing her neck.

She looked surprised to see me. "What are you doing home?" she asked.

"It's night," I said. "It's night and I came home."

I waited for something to happen. The man's hand was on my mother's breast. He didn't stop kissing her neck, but she was looking at me.

After I got off the phone with Gene I drank some vodka but couldn't sleep from the pain in my mouth. I tried to call Basille but got his voicemail. I left him a message: "Just checking on Mom," I said. "And a job. Give me a call." I sat in the chair by the window and read a book about Chet Baker that I took from Meg's shelf. Mostly I looked at the photos, black-and-whites of a man born in Yale, Oklahoma, thin and pale, losing teeth, sick from shooting drugs— this must have been what my father looked like before he died. We used to tell people Chet Baker was our father. Mom always listened to his records. Some nights we sat in the living room, listening to *Live in Montmartre, Night Bird, Conception, I Remember You*.

I ate some soup, head down in the bowl. Then I sat in a chair by a lamp, next to bookshelves. There were no other books worth reading. In the bathroom I took four Ibuprofen and moved back to the chair by the window and saw a dog crossing Crowdus. The dog stopped and pawed at something under a fence. I decided to take a walk. Outside, in the coldness of night, I passed a few people who I imagined were headed home, leaning into the wind.

There was a man down the block in a Mavericks jersey and baggy pants, wearing a stocking cap, clapping his gloved hands and singing "Under the Boardwalk." He pointed at me as I walked by, still singing and smiling, then wagged his finger at me as if I were in trouble. In front of a diner, napkins were flying in the wind. A truck, gutted and stripped, was parked on the corner of Good Latimer and Elm. Nobody was around. I stopped and took it in. For a moment nothing seemed to move. I turned and headed back only to see a woman limping into the street, carrying bags in each hand. She was headed south toward Main but was watching me.

Snow on the roofs of buildings gleamed in the moonlight. From the rear fender of a parked car along Elm hung little icicles that sparkled. I walked past the store windows, past small mounds of dirty snow along the street. A dog was barking from somewhere above me, in one of the apartments, but besides that there was no traffic and little noise. Deep Ellum in the winter was asleep. I headed back to Meg's.

When I got back upstairs to the apartment I sat down and closed my eyes. I kept Meg's coat on. I drifted off for a while, and when I opened my eyes I heard a noise at the door, keys jingling, and then the door opened and Meg was standing there. She held two sacks of groceries, put them down on the table and came over and hugged me for a long time. She rested her head on my shoulder.

"I'm so glad to see you," Meg said. "Why are you wearing my coat?"

"I gave mine away."

"I'm glad you're back. Your face looks swollen, though. What happened to your cheek?"

"Bad tooth. Maybe a cavity. I guess I need to see a dentist."

"You should call one before it gets infected. Have you talked to Mom?"

"I talked to Gene," I said. "Who's this guy you've been with?"

"Nobody. Seriously. So, you want to go out for a drink? There's a jazz place down on Elm Street that's good Thursdays."

Her hair was shorter and dyed darker. I helped her put up groceries, then drank some vodka and we talked for a while. She looked tired but somehow still seemed energetic. Fatigue and tension made her eager to talk. She avoided eye contact, but when her eyes met mine something filled the space between us. "I remember when you texted me your first night in Chicago," she said. "You wrote: 'Chicago feels like it's an invention of people from lost places.'"

"I don't remember," I said.

She sat at the window, looking outside. There was frost on the sill, which made me want to stay in.

"Have you talked to Basille?" Meg asked.

"I just left him a message. I haven't heard back."

Our younger brother lived alone in an apartment building, upstairs from a small picture framing shop on Pacific Avenue, where he worked four days a week. He made a marginal income, as he called it, considering his degree was in music. On Monday nights he played piano at a retirement home in Plano and on weekends he sometimes played trumpet at a jazz club on Commerce, downtown.

He was a loner, even worse than me. He had a high I.Q. At the age of eleven, he became the youngest contestant to win the National Geographic Bee, in Washington D.C. and collapsed into tears for two days afterwards because he didn't feel happy about winning. One day his teacher called our mother because he rolled around on the classroom floor, speaking strange languages. Our mother said he was doing it for attention. There were other odd quirks. He walked backwards through doorways. He had no clear explanation for this. Our mother brought in a psychic, a woman she'd found in the yellow pages. The woman carried candles and circled his bed, but that didn't work. Nothing worked.

When he was a teenager he thought he wanted to one day be a surgeon specializing in the surgery of hands. He was interested in bones and joints, the way things connected. He landed a half academic half music scholarship at the University of Texas down in Austin. Since Meg and I never went to college, Basille was the first in our family to earn a college degree. But for a time when he was little he never spoke. Meg and I could never tell if he was happy or sad. One day Meg and I took him to the backyard, pretending to be his parents. We read him Russian fairy tales and had a tea party with him. We waited for him to say something. We were always waiting for him to laugh or to cry.

Meg drove us to a jazz club. It wasn't too far, just down Elm. We went under the freeway and turned into the parking lot. The guy playing piano was a black guy with an afro and beard, an older man. He wore jeans and an old shirt with his sleeves rolled up. There were empty beer bottles on the piano and the guy smoked and hunched over the keys while he played. He really got into it. Meg and I smoked and had a couple of drinks as we listened to him.

At the bar I saw Meg reach for something in her purse—a pill—and then take it with her drink.

I leaned over the table and asked what it was.

"Nothing," she said. "Xanax."

She sat back and watched the guy. I was overcome with a sudden sadness. When we got back to the apartment I watched her undress and then sit in the kitchen and give herself allergy shots in the leg. She dipped cotton into a bottle of alcohol and swabbed an area on her upper thigh. There was a tiny vial of serum for her allergy to grass and weeds. She filled a syringe from the vial and stuck the needle into her thigh. She swabbed the area again with cotton and discarded the needle into a plastic waste dispenser. She claimed she didn't want to go to the clinic and get the shot every week because the clinic was on the west side and fighting traffic wasn't worth it. But I was skeptical.

She kept her prescription box of needles in a glass cabinet with her dishes, like she was hiding them there, and I wondered if that was what the earlier visitor Charlie was looking for. I asked her about this, why she felt the need to hide them.

"I hide coffee too," she said.

In the bathroom she ran bathwater while I stayed in the kitchen and sliced an orange in half with a knife. Then I went into the bathroom and sat on the floor while she was in the tub. I pulled my knees to my chest and watched her.

25

"Do you have to work tomorrow?" I asked.

"I didn't tell you, but I quit that job at the clinic."

"Why?"

"Long story, but my boss was basically a stupid fuck. So what are your plans? Are you going back to Chicago? You seemed to like it there."

I didn't tell her that in Chicago I'd walked home from work many nights in blowing snow when the wind chill was below zero and I didn't have gloves because I'd loaned them to a girl at work who'd forgotten hers. Or how the first two weeks in Chicago I'd slept on the floor because I didn't own a bed. I didn't tell her I hadn't been to a dentist in years because of no insurance. Or the times our landlord, an old Puerto Rican guy named Andres who walked with a limp, laughed at me when I asked him about the bugs in the apartment. Or how Andres made racial slurs when he fixed the bathroom sink. I didn't mention the time I hurt my hand when I punched a wall at work because my boss threatened to fire me if I didn't start washing my white collared work shirt and look more presentable. "This is restaurant business," he said. "Either you wash your shirts, or you find somewhere else to work." And I never mentioned the times I thought of her, all the nights I worried she was with one of her abusive boyfriends.

"I don't want to think about anything right now," I said. "Maybe I'll stay for a while and work. When I get enough money I might think about going back to Chicago. I don't know."

She took a long breath and sunk into the bath. There were times like this, on occasion, when she held expressions that reminded me of our childhood. I could see in her face the way she looked when we were younger, before any of us left home. There was a time we stayed in a tent in her bedroom for four days in a row, coming out only to use the bathroom. Our mother brought us our meals. We played word games. We listened to records and wrote our names with colored markers on notebook paper. This was how I preferred to think of her.

She leaned back, resting her arm on the side of the tub, relaxing. "I knew you'd find your way in here," she said.

I sucked the juice from the flesh of the orange.

6

Our real father died when I was five. Our mother found him one morning. He was a drug addict. We were living in a suburb at the time, in a little apartment. Meg has a much better memory of him than I do. She was the oldest. She says he was funny and smart and that he played the piano for us and took us out to eat with his friends. My only memory of him is vague—I was sitting on a divan in someone's crummy apartment, looking up at him while he smoked and laughed and moved his hands around as he talked. He didn't have any teeth from the drug use. He looked old, talked loud and I remember he sometimes broke into fits of laughter. Our mother said he struggled with his drug problem most of his adult life. In photos his hands look bony and aged, his face pale and sunken. A few years later Gene came along.

When our mother first started dating Gene I immersed myself in a project that involved documenting the behavior of insects that were collecting under the cabinets in the kitchen. I did this secretly, or at least as secretly as I could, without telling our mother. During the afternoons Meg and I were at home a lot by ourselves, so when Meg pulled me into her bedroom and explored my body she could do so in privacy. Our mother took Basille, a toddler at the time, with her whenever she left the house during the day. When I wasn't with Meg I watched the behavior of insects. I was way more interested in this project than anything else at that time, although I was not happy. Maybe this was because our mother was staying out late most nights and that for the past year or so I'd seen her bring home different men. Meg and Basille both seemed happy though.

During the summer months it was common for lots of insects to get into the house. I sat in the dark cabinet under the sink with my yellow legal pad and pen and counted them. There was generally only one kind, brown beetle-looking bugs with wings that looked like roaches. They came in through cracks in the kitchen window and bathroom and garage. I spent days watching them—crouched in the cabinet under the sink, in the hall bathroom or under the workbench in the garage, where all sorts of lint and dirt and sawdust collected around me.

In the hall bathroom I sat on the floor next to the toilet, where the baseboard was rotted and coming apart. My mother was worried about me since I told her I was having stomach issues and kept myself locked in there for so long. I crouched down with a magnifying glass and my yellow legal pad of paper, looking for bugs. The way the baseboard was rotting, I suspected we had termites, but when I showed it to Gene, he didn't think so.

"Looks like water damage," he said. "I'm sure it's not termites, but we'll have to call somebody to come out regardless."

In the bathroom I was able to document seven bugs, two of which were spiders. Their behavior was independent. There was no touching or bumping into other insects. They looked for dark places, left each other alone. I was amazed by how disinterested they were in each other and me. They merely monitored my movement. I had to be still, particularly around the spiders. Perfectly still. Not a movement. I worried they could hear me breathing.

In the garage I had even worse luck. I crouched down underneath the workbench. I counted mostly spiders there, and more flies, some of which were dead. I collected them and kept them in an old Dutch Masters cigar box. It was important work for me, work that gave me a sense of control, a sense of independence, something to keep my mind occupied. The insects struggled to survive. They relied on instinct.

One afternoon Meg came in and found me. "Come to my room," she said.

"I'm working. I still have to do chores."

"I hate you," she said.

Later Basille wandered in, carrying his toy plane and making engine noises with his mouth. He got on his hands and knees and crawled under the workbench with me. When our mother arrived calling his name, frantic and near hysterics, she immediately became angry. She made Basille crawl out and then picked him up and held him.

"Gideon Gray," she told me. "You're in big trouble when Gene gets home."

Back then I had lots of chores: taking out the garbage, feeding and putting water out for the dog, picking up my room. Sometimes our mother told me to help her clean the house. She'd put Olde English furniture polish on a rag and have me wipe down the kitchen table, the baseboards, frames around doorways. Meg had chores too, but sometimes I surprised her by picking up her room for her or already having all the trash taken out by the time she got home. I always beat her home from school because I rode a bike and she walked and sometimes stopped at a friend's house before coming home. I liked to tell her that everything was already done when she got home. Our mother would know I worked hard and hopefully Meg would appreciate it.

The most crucial of my chores was making sure the windows and door of the shed out back were always shut tight and locked so that opossums or mice or rats wouldn't get in and eat the dog food. Our mother liked to keep the dog food and water in there, where our dog usually slept since we didn't keep him in the house. In the summer the shade kept him cooler and in the winter it was warmer. Our mother was strict about this since one summer we had problems with opossums coming around the shed. Sometimes at night I'd wake up thinking I'd forgotten to close the windows.

I don't remember much when Basille was a baby. I do remember living in a condemned building in a bad part of Dallas. I remember trying to catch crawdads in a creek with a boy who lived in the apartment upstairs. Sometimes we could hear noises from his apartment that sounded like a wrench hitting something metal. We heard footsteps on the ceiling when we tried to sleep. The boy once pulled his shirt up and showed me a horrible scar spread across his stomach where hot grease had spilled on him.

I remember the sound the pipes made when you turned on the water in the tub. Meg said it sounded like me when I was crying. I remember the tiny apartment where our mother sat in front of the TV, smoking cigarette after cigarette. The whole room filled with blue smoke. I remember sitting in the principal's office at school, being sent home for head lice. The boy sitting next to me kept touching my head. He said my hair felt like the inside of a dog's ear.

When we moved out to the country, we had the same plumbing problem. The pipes made noise when the water turned on, just like in our old apartment. The plumber, a large man with a plaster cast on his wrist, told our mother his teenage son had dirty magazines strewn about his bedroom. "The boy's a troublemaker," he said. He sounded exhausted and sad. He stared at the metal tool in his hand. "I've given up on him and his mother."

It was a strange time. I was shocked, if not disturbed, by how often Basille cried. He was barely walking then. Crying, he would walk around the house in a diaper that sagged. Nobody could figure out what was wrong with him. Our mother changed his diaper. She fed him, played with him, tried everything. Eventually we guessed he was mimicking the sound of the pipes from the tub.

Basille's behavior spoiled something. A great uneasiness filled the house so that our mother and Gene stayed out later at night, leaving Meg to watch me and Basille.

One day I heard her scream from the backyard. When I went out, there was a dead rat in the shed. Our dog had killed it and dragged it in there. The dog sat panting proudly. I tried to pick up the rat but Rufus picked it up in his mouth and ran past me. I had to go inside and get pieces of bologna to lure the dog away so he'd drop the rat. Then I picked up the rat with the shovel and dumped it along the side of the road.

Soon Meg developed strange habits. During bad thunderstorms she covered all the mirrors in the house with sheets. She said seeing her reflection meant bad luck. She spent a great deal of time outside. She once found a nest of bluish eggs in some tall grass across Fulton Road. We guessed they belonged to a duck that had wandered off. One of the eggs was cracked. I ran my finger over the crack, which opened up the egg and I saw bloody flesh. Meg kept the eggs in the shed until Gene found them and got mad at her.

This was around the time Meg and I stayed with our aunt, our mother's sister, for a few months. Neither of us were getting along with Gene or our mother. Our mother accused Meg of stealing things. In Meg's room she found cigarettes, a joint, a pair of fishnet stockings and towel from a Holiday Inn. Our first night at our aunt's house, I sat at the window looking out at the street below. I was twelve. I waited for Meg to come home from her job at Coit's Drive-In, where she wore roller skates and served cherry cokes and burgers. It was getting dark out and I went to our room to try to sleep a while. As I lay there I kept hearing the boy who lived downstairs. He was crying out.

"It's that boy again," my aunt said. "That boy, there's something wrong with him. Just so you know. Blind and deformed or something. I never heard noises like that. Why are you acting so sad?"

I didn't say anything or look up at her. I was lying on my back with my arm over my face.

"Charlie's coming over," she said. "We'll be in my room with the music on in case you decide you want to go somewhere. I mean that's fine with me. Just so you know. If you go out lock the door when you leave. I have to work early."

After she left I got a can of spray paint out of the closet. I crouched and sprayed into a little plastic baggie and huffed. I sprayed and huffed again. I closed my eyes and lay down for a while. I liked hiding, sitting alone in the closet. When Meg and I were younger we'd hide in our closet, under the bed, sometimes in the basement. We did that for hours.

After a while I went outside and sat at the bottom of the stairs and smoked. The woman from downstairs was sweeping her porch. She was Hispanic, maybe Puerto Rican. She was wearing old jeans and men's work boots.

"You're staying with that girl upstairs," she said.

I mashed out my cigarette and didn't say anything. It was cold. I sat there and put my face down in my coat. The collar was warm and lined with fur.

"I've seen her. I know what she's up to."

I closed my eyes. Maybe I fell asleep for a minute, because when I opened them the woman was leaning against the wall, still talking. She was saying, "He almost drowned in the river. He makes noises in his sleep when his head hurts. Don't let him scare you, though. You tired? You want some coffee, I bet. Got some I just made."

I stood with my hands in Meg's coat pockets and saw the boy's face, her son, through the window. He was sitting slumped in a

31

wheelchair. I looked at the woman and she seemed to be studying me.

"Inside," she said. "You alright?"

I followed her into her apartment. The room was dimly lit. I went over to the boy while the woman went to the kitchen. He was small, maybe nine years old. He was sitting with his head over to one side. Blind. His open mouth collected saliva as he breathed, making gurgling noises. His head moved in my direction as if he knew I was there. He put his hand to his head, his mouth still open.

"Paolo won't hurt you," the woman said. She was standing in front of a mirror, painting her lips red.

I touched his face as he made noises with his mouth. I felt his jaw, his mouth. I saw little teeth through mucus. He reached for me and touched Meg's coat, the fur collar.

The woman was at the couch, fluffing two fat pillows when the boy started crying out loudly. She came over and touched his brow, knelt down and whispered in his ear, but he kept crying out.

"I have to go," I said.

"Everything is fine," the woman said, looking at me. I wasn't sure if she was talking to me or to her son. "We're fine. Everything is fine."

"I have to go," I said again, then I turned and left. I could hear her saying that over and over, "Everything is fine."

I hurried back upstairs to my aunt's apartment and went into Meg's room. I sat at the window and smoked and waited for her to come home. My last cigarette was broken. I took off my coat and hung it up in the closet. There were some clothes on the floor. I folded them and put them on the dresser. Then I got into her bed with my clothes on and finally fell asleep until late in the night.

The room was dark when Meg came in. She came over and sat on the edge of the bed. She pulled off her T-shirt and got under the covers. Her hands were cold on my back. Her mouth was on my neck. I could smell perfume and liquor on her body, her hair. I didn't ask her anything, where she was or who she was with. She pulled off my shirt and pinched me, laughing quietly. The boy downstairs was crying out. We listened to him. She put her hand down my jeans. We pulled the covers over us.

When Meg got out of the bath she went straight to bed. I stayed up, sipping vodka and going through the classifieds in the newspaper. Around three in the morning I turned off the lamp and tiptoed into Meg's room. I got into bed with her and fell fast asleep. Most of the night I slept with my head under her arm. I dreamed of other worlds, medieval ruined towns, castles, low skies with racing clouds. I was walking down a trail of rubble. It was hot and windy, nothing around me. I kept walking and saw our mother in the distance. I approached her, shielding myself from the wind, but she was waving me away, saying, *Go away, go away.*

When I woke in the morning Meg wasn't there. My mouth was killing me. In the mirror I saw how swollen my jaw was. My face and hair looked dirty. I took a shower, got dressed and found Meg's coffee under the sink. Brewed a pot and sat in the living room for a while. The room was bathed in morning light. The street below was dead. After a while Meg texted me: *Back later and we'll go to Mom's.*

I ate a bagel and tried to go back to sleep, drifting off and on. Then I heard Meg come in telling me my face looked worse. "Let me give you the name of my dentist." I got out of bed and looked at myself in the mirror. It made me look sick and weird. Meg gave me the number to her dentist and I spoke to a receptionist. Due to a cancellation they were able to get me in for an appointment at 4:30 that afternoon.

"I'm not going to Mom's," Meg said. "I can't go. I don't want to go."

"Why not?"

"We'll just fight. I can't do that to Mom right now. She'll be worse if I go, trust me. Tell her I have an appointment with the doctor that I've already rescheduled. You can take my car."

33

I didn't argue with her. There was no point. I headed out of the city in her Toyota. The sun was out but it was still cold. Our mother and Gene lived fifty miles east, in a different county. This is where we grew up, in a strange little town called Red Owl, a town of blue-collar workers—welders and farmers, machinists and retired railroad workers.

Our mother found comfort in the quiet of a rural town. Throughout her life, she never slept enough. I always wondered if this brought on her depression and other frequent ailments. She was often coughing, though I attributed it to her constant smoking. She was pale and sick a great deal when I was a kid living at home. When she was sick she wanted us out of the house. At her worst she was silent and bedridden, but mostly just irritable. Meg and I would sit at the foot of her bed examining her little medicine bottles and she'd tell us to get out of the house for a while, go down to the creek or something.

Then, out of nowhere, she got better. This happened every so often, she started feeling better and all of a sudden she was out of bed and dressed and rushing around to go somewhere. I never understood what brought her out of such misery and self-loathing. Gene used to say she was bi-polar, though she always denied that. That may have been what some of her meds were for.

Her father, my grandfather, was a butcher at the supermarket. He had a gambling problem. When I turned eighteen he took me to Lone Star Park for horseracing. He taught me how to handicap horses in a racing form. My grandfather was a sort of enigma to me. For a few years after the Korean War, he worked the shipyards on the Boston waterfront. After that he inherited some land and moved his family down to Texas, where he took up work as a butcher. He let me scrape the butcher blocks with a brush until they were clean. My mother rarely talked about him, and he rarely talked about anything other than gambling, horses or the horse trainers he knew. He had an intensity about him that I was sometimes afraid of. His expressions gave him away. He'd sit in his pickup truck and smoke and you could tell he was pissed off at something. His story about my mother's nervous breakdown went like this: "Your mother had a breakdown once. That's all you need to know. It was a goddamn mess. Good thing she got better."

He died of a stroke when I was twenty. There was a small graveside service at the cemetery outside of town. Veterans showed up and saluted the flag, shook my hand and told me what a courageous and strong grandfather I had. He was a man of adventure, they told me. A man of strong work ethic and good morals. I pretended I knew what they were talking about. My mother and her sister knew a lot of people at the service I'd never seen before. My mother never cried. As often as she was depressed, I never saw my mother cry.

I drove Meg's Toyota east, out of the city forty miles toward Red Owl, into prairieland, past farmland and open fields. Past the El Dorado Motor Lodge turning onto Fulton Road. I drove past Nick's Garage and then past Ellis Park, where Basille and I used to play football. When I pulled into the drive, Gene and Basille came out to meet me. Basille was unshaven, wearing an old torn coat and jeans.

"What happened to your face?" Gene asked.

"Cavity or something. I'm going to the dentist today."

"It looks bad," he said. "All swollen. You've got an infection of some sort."

"Mom's in bed," Basille said. "She wanted to be left alone, but we told her you were in town."

We went inside to the bedroom. I stood in the doorway. Our mother lay in bed on her side, under the covers, eyes barely open. I wondered if she'd been drinking. Meg told me that before her breakdown our mother often sat outside in her bathrobe drinking vodka cranberries until she could barely walk back in. She was drunk a lot when I was younger, but nobody ever addressed it. I never did like the parties she and Gene had, their motorcycle friends, their staying away from home until late in the night. At some point it became routine.

Basille and Gene sat in chairs at the foot of the bed. I leaned down and kissed her on the cheek and sat in the chair beside her. She wanted the light off, so there was only a small lamp on in the corner of the room. I asked if we could open the drapes, but she wanted them closed.

"How was your flight?" she asked.

"Good," I said. "No problems."

"Where's Meg?"

"At the doctor. She said she's sorry she couldn't make it."

I was never very good at lying for Meg. Our mother knew this, I think, by the way she looked at me, though she remained silent about it. I gave her the snow globe that I'd bought at the antique store near Meg's place. She looked at it, still on her side. "Christmas was last month," she said.

She reigned in that bed, I thought. Wallowing in self-pity while we all gathered around.

"Your mother is depressed," Gene said, shifting in his chair. He blinked rapidly. "She's on new medication with side effects—vomiting, nausea and dry mouth—but for the most part she's doing better."

Gene's hands trembled from breathing aluminum and asbestos. He had a nervous habit of fidgeting in his chair, talking constantly, almost always moving, walking from room to room, somehow being everywhere at once. He got up, went to the kitchen and came right back with a glass of water. He talked as he brought the glass of water to her mouth. "Her stomach has been upset," he said. "Juice, soda, ginger ale, tea—none of it sounds good to her. Her doctor thinks she might need to go inpatient at St. Francis if things don't get better. I told him we're all here to make sure she stays safe and goddamned if she gets admitted to any mental hospital. She's getting better, though. Look at her."

Her eyes were swollen. She tried to smile. Basille's mind was wandering. He sat with his hands behind his head, staring distantly into the wall behind me. I asked him whether he was going back to work in the next day or so.

"I'm off for a week," he said. "I thought about hanging out with you while you're here."

"That's fine," Gene said. "Except we'll need your help around here. Sometimes I need a break."

"You took a break last night," Basille said.

"I just want to be left alone," our mother said.

"This is not easy for anyone," Gene told Basille. "I'd like to see a show of hands of anyone who thinks this is easy."

"You want to know what would make me happy?" our mother said. "For Meg to be here. And Gideon, I hope you can spend some time with Gene. You never spent time together. That would make me happy."

I looked at Basille, who was pulling on his bottom lip, staring at the floor, trying not to laugh.

Gene leaned forward and stared at me. "Fine with me if it's fine with you."

"Fine with me," I said.

Gene kept looking at me. "Gideon," he said. "My own mother just turned seventy-nine. She's had Alzheimer's and we had to put her in a nursing home for a few months. She's a woman of few words. She sits in a chair with her head lolling to one side. Suffers bad dreams. Incontinence. Sudden bowel movements. They pay the staff shit. Eight bucks an hour. Those shit slingers would let her rot if they could. She doesn't sit in the day room with the other residents. She keeps to herself in her room, in the dark, with the drapes drawn. When I visit her she doesn't look at me. She sits in her chair and drools and stares at the goddamn floor."

"Why are you telling me this?" I said.

"I'm speaking to everyone. You're just the person I'm looking at. If I turn my head and look at everyone I end up losing track of whatever I'm trying to say. Don't take it personally. This is a hard time for everyone. Bad things are happening in Red Owl. The town's cursed these days. I believe it. People are sick and dying all around us."

"I'd like to be alone now," our mother said.

I stared at her, zoning out Gene's constant babbling. His voice was aimless and nonstop, vibrations coming from a whole other entity, a voice I'd learned over the years to tolerate and ignore. Basille stared at the floor. Gene quit talking and the room fell silent for the first time. The phone on the table beside Gene rang and he flinched, jerking his head to look.

My tooth was killing me. It was time to go.

Our mother drove us to Amarillo once. I didn't know where we were going. Sometimes she did that, put us in the car and said we were going on a road trip somewhere. On that trip our car started smoking under the hood, so we pulled into a gas station off I-40. Two men had rags in their pockets and grease all over their clothes. Inside the station, the radio was playing country and western music. The woman behind the counter looked worried. She smiled and served us coffee while we waited. An elderly woman came in and bought a cup of coffee. She sat beside us and looked out the window.

"Bad storm's coming," she told us, demonstrating a rainstorm with her hands. Then she talked about her cat. Her hands shook as she held her coffee. From time to time she said something about a dead armadillo on the gravel road to her house. It started to drizzle. Outside dark clouds were approaching.

"Armadillos carry leprosy," she said. "Did you know that?" She smiled at me as she spoke. "A long time ago, my husband had one as a pet. Used to walk it on a leash."

The guy from the garage came in and said our car wouldn't be ready. They had to order parts from Amarillo. It would be a few days. He said there was a motel down the street.

We were at the beginning or in the middle of nowhere. I was six years old and I was looking at a woman.

-8-

Basille drove us back to Dallas and dropped me off at Meg's apartment. The first thing I wanted to do was find a job. Other than Basille, I had no serious leads. I walked down Crowdus and over to Elm, where I bought a newspaper. There was a homeless man with a thick beard leaning against a lamppost, his hands in the pockets of his coat. I walked past and ducked into a small coffee shop, where I spent an hour sifting through the classifieds. There wasn't much of anything.

I called a friend of mine, Colin Ward, and asked if he knew of anything. His family had money and I'd done some painting work for his dad before I left for Chicago. In addition to his job as a big wheel for a local TV station, Mr. Ward owned four or five rental houses and needed someone to go in and repaint the walls and do small repair work, so I'd earned some extra cash that way. Mr. Ward was also a musician and one time even played rhythm guitar with Huey Lewis and the News during a show at one of the Indian casinos. He had connections, something I admired about him. He'd traveled abroad and around the country on business. These days he was making a documentary with his brothers, his "life project" as he called it, reenacting the death of their great-grandfather, a Union soldier and wagon freighter from Oklahoma who was killed by Indians at Massey Creek up near Enid. I saw footage at Colin's house before I left for Chicago. One of Mr. Ward's brother's was a wrangler who supplied the rolling stock and western outfits they all wore. Mr. Ward made Colin be an extra in the film so he had to dress as a cowboy and hold a rifle. They ran his picture in the Enid newspaper, but Colin told me he didn't give a shit because he was high the whole time.

"I don't know of any jobs," Colin told me over the phone.

"Why don't you stop by and we'll go over to my dad's?" I knew what this meant, though—Colin was looking for pot.

"I don't have any pot," I told him.

"I wasn't even thinking about that," he said, laughing. "Fucking Gideon, man."

"So your dad's at home or what? You think he's got work?"

"I told you, I don't know. Stop by my place."

When we were in high school, one time Colin and I went fishing at a pond near his parents' house. We caught some perch with the fishing rods we'd taken from Mr. Ward's shed. We tossed the fish back into the cold water and watched them swim under. That same night for dinner Mrs. Ward made a type of chicken and rice dish and Mr. Ward let us drink liqueur in the den with him while we listened to him discuss his plans for Colin to eventually go to law school, which Colin had no interest in. Mr. Ward was always nice to me, and though he knew my family didn't have money he never treated me unkind or made me feel less fortunate.

"You should go into music," he'd always tell me. "Or maybe business. You like numbers, right? You could go into accounting."

I knew he was just trying to get me interested in something. I always suspected he felt sorry for me.

When I got off the phone with Colin I borrowed Meg's car and drove over to his apartment, but he wasn't home. I kept knocking on the door. I texted him: *Colin, I'm here. Where are you?*

I went back and sat in the car and waited. I was freezing. I turned on the engine and put the heater on high. My tooth was hurting and I kept opening my mouth and looking in the rearview mirror.

Twenty minutes later Colin finally texted back: *Sorry man, had to take off. Problems with the girlfriend. Hit me up later and let me know if you score any pot.*

Later Basille showed up at Meg's apartment. He took forever climbing the stairs because he paused every other one, some sort of weird phobia he had. It made no sense. Meg asked how our trip was.

"She wants you to visit," I said. "She wants all of us there."

Meg put on her jacket and looked in the pockets. "Where are my cigarettes?"

Basille lay down on the divan and closed his eyes while I brushed my teeth. I looked at myself in the mirror and felt my jaw.

Then Meg drove me to the dentist's office near downtown and said she had some business to attend to.

"What business?" I asked her.

"Nothing important, really. Don't worry about it."

"Just curious."

"Gideon, don't worry. Can you catch the bus back?"

She drove off in a hurry. I had to wait a long time in the dentist's office, flipping through women's magazines. When they finally called me, the dental assistant reclined me in the chair and prodded around in my mouth with a sharp metal instrument. She was an older woman who never smiled. She asked what I did for a living and I told her nothing. She didn't say anything more after that. The dentist was a younger guy, pale-skinned and clean-shaven, wearing round glasses. He commented on my swollen jaw while I stared into the yellow light of the lamp above.

"It's certainly swollen," he said. He hummed while he rooted around in my mouth. Finally he flipped off the lamp and told me I had an abscessed tooth that needed to be extracted. "We can drain it and you can come back, or we can extract it now."

I told him I wanted it done now and he seemed pleased. He muttered something to his assistant and turned the lamp back on. He shot my gum with a needle to numb it. The whole process didn't take long. When it was all over he prescribed an antibiotic and Hydrocodone for pain.

"Be careful with this stuff," he told me.

I filled the prescriptions at the CVS down the street then walked to the bus stop. When I got back to Meg's apartment she was still gone. Basille was writing on a yellow legal pad, rewriting entire conversations he'd had with a former girlfriend.

"She never cheated," he said. "She was only around for a couple of months."

"What was her name?"

"Petia."

"Russian?"

"Bulgarian. Grad student at SMU. Crazy fucking hot."

We went out for a beer. We walked south on Crowdus. Always south. There was nothing north of the building but an old school with boarded-up windows and an empty lot. The sun was out but the wind was cold. A man was unloading boxes from a truck on the corner. He wore a hoodie under a heavy coat, whistling as he carried boxes to the door of a brick building. Basille was walking with his hands in his pockets.

"I think Meg's dating a dealer," he said.

"What are you talking about?"

"Some guy Axel, I think he's a dealer. Not sure what he's dealing though."

"How do you know this?"

"It's why Mom had her breakdown." His voice was shaky from the cold walk.

"Mom's always had problems," I said. "Are you saying there was some specific event?"

"They had a fight, Mom and Meg. This Axel guy was in some sort of trouble and Meg loaned him money. She had to borrow it from Gene and Mom and still hasn't paid them back."

"They wouldn't loan her money. They don't have enough."

"She lied to them," he said. "Told them she was behind on her rent and about to be evicted from her place. Gene called her a fist fucker and wrote out a check."

"Meg has syringes," I said. "A whole box of them. For allergy shots."

We went into The Prophet Bar. We sat at the bar and ordered beers and Basille ordered a sandwich. The bartender had purple-black hair and tattoos on both her arms. She didn't smile when she served us and seemed focused on some interior presence.

The Mavs were playing on TV. I drank my beer and watched the game while Basille picked apart his sandwich, eating the pickles and lettuce before the meat. As he ate he told me that Gene was helping a friend of his, a retired foundry worker, sell scrap metal to recycling plants. Apparently they were doing pretty well. This friend had a couple of young Hispanic guys working for him. Basille said our mother thought Gene's friend was sketchy and didn't want Gene working with him. "I heard them argue about it. If Gene's friend gets audited he's fucked."

"How do you know all this?"

He wiped his mouth with a napkin. "When are they concerned about who hears their fights?"

I watched the bartender. The place wasn't very crowded and she was down at the other end of the bar, talking to an older woman who sat alone.

"What is it with Gene always calling people weird names?" Basille said. "Have you ever noticed nobody's ever just an asshole? Everyone's a fist fucker or a shit stabber."

"I remember he called Mr. Sangupta a goddamn foreigner."

"He walks too fast and hunches forward when he walks. He fidgets. Blinks a lot. Doesn't close the door when he takes a piss."

"What else?"

"There's always dried spittle in the corners of his mouth. He hacks up phlegm. He walks around the house too fast, hunched forward, without a shirt on."

Meg texted me: *Where'd u guys go?*

I texted back: *Getting a beer at Prophet. Be back soon.*

Meg: *I have to go out for a bit, but I'll be at Puig's party later. Meet me there. I left his address on the table for u.*

"Meg has to go out for a while."

"She's with Axel," Basille said. "I'll bet anything."

I could feel the Hydrocodone kicking in.

Meg's boyfriends were always older. There was something about older loser types she liked. One time when I was around thirteen, Meg told me her boyfriend Jack was coming over and they were going somewhere. Jack was about twenty and she was sixteen. He worked at a metal building supply company his dad owned on the outskirts of town. Meg said I could get a job there when I was older as long as I was nice to Jack and acted interested.

That day he came over I didn't look at her or say anything. After she left I went into the garage and got my fishing pole and bait. I walked down the street. It was summer and already hot, and by the time I got to the pond I was already sweating. I sat down and opened my tackle box, put the bait on the line. I fished for a while until another kid showed up, an Indian kid from the tribal housing district nearby. He had buckteeth and carried a fishing pole and a brown paper sack.

"Hey," he said. "You catch anything?"

"Not yet," I said.

"I caught a big catfish over here the other day," he said. "That ain't a good spot where you're at."

I reeled my line in and carried my pole and tackle box over next to him. He pulled a bottle of something from his sack. "You want a drink?" he asked.

I shook my head. Then he got some porn magazines from the sack and showed them to me. The magazines were old.

"These are good," the kid said.

There were pictures of naked women touching themselves. There were at least eleven or twelve of these magazines, and we looked at them for a long time. We never fished. The kid took a drink from the bottle and made a face. He handed me the bottle and said it was whiskey. I was thirsty, so I took a drink.

"It burns," he said. "You got a boner?"

"Shit," I said. I took another drink, then another.

The boy said he had more magazines back at his house and some dirty movies his mother and her boyfriend had. "You want to come over?" We packed up and started walking up the trail that led to the road, but I was dizzy and feeling sick. I had to stop walking, and the kid looked at me. "What's wrong?" he said.

"I feel bad," I said, holding my stomach. "I better go home."

"I'll be here tomorrow," the kid said from behind. "Okay, kid?"

I kept walking until I finally made it home. When I got there, Jack's car was in the driveway. I put my tackle box and fishing pole in the garage and went straight inside to my room and laid down on my bed. I could hear my sister in the next room getting fucked by her boyfriend. Hearing her was wonderful.

9

When we left The Prophet Bar, Basille told me he had a lead for a job. We stopped by to see a friend of his, a guy named Rick, who owned a guitar shop with his brother. Both of them played in an alt-country band called Spoon Nostril. I'd seen them play a couple of times at The Prophet Bar before I'd left for Chicago. They played originals but also covers of Hank Williams Jr. and Steve Earle and Johnny Cash.

"Damn good guitar player," Basille said.

Meg actually dated Rick a few years earlier, though I'd never officially met him. She'd gone to Austin with him for a music festival where his band was playing. This was before Spoon Nostril, when Rick was playing in a psychobilly band called Truck Stop Pussy with three other guys who did lots of coke right before they went on stage. They became a hit with local punks when the singer, who called himself Fuckhead Red, took off all his clothes at the end of a show and grunted into the microphone. During one of the shows Meg saw in Fort Worth, Fuckhead Red got arrested for indecent exposure and Rick ended up bailing him out of jail. Fuckhead Red never paid Rick back, so Rick left the band and put together Spoon Nostril. Rick wrote a song for Meg called "Twenty-First Century Girl" that he sang the first night Spoon Nostril performed at a biker rally out in Carrolton.

When we got to Rick's apartment, he was restringing his Gretsch. Basille introduced us and he asked if I played.

"A little," I said. "I grew up playing some."

He had an acoustic Martin that he wanted me to play. The neck felt good. I strummed around on it for a while, finger-picking early Dylan, Cat Stevens, Neil Young.

"Nice," he said. "I may have something soon. We're getting overloaded on lessons, so I might want you to help out some with those also."

"That'd be good," I said.

Rick's girlfriend Marci gave Basille some Ecstasy and we each took one. Rick told me about Spoon Nostril and showed me some of his lyrics.

"Here's a song I wrote about Meg," he said, handing me the notebook. I read the lyrics scrawled in blue ink:

> *She's got me confused and blind,*
> *I'm going blind!*
> *I don't know what to do, who to do,*
> *Lost my mind in Deep Ellum,*
> *Lost my mind in the gutter,*
> *In the sky she's like no other,*
> *She likes Tantric masturbation,*
> *A twenty-first century fuck goddes*

"Nice," I lied, handing the notebook back to Rick. "I hope she liked it."

He kept telling me about his band. When I felt the Ecstasy kicking in I told him Basille and I needed to go but that we loved hanging out with him and gave him my cell number.

"You'll love Rick," Basille said on the walk from his apartment.

We went into a crummy topless bar not far from Rick's apartment and drank a pitcher of beer. We sat at a table near the stage and flirted with the waitress, who told us her name was Z.

"Short for Zoe or Zelly or something?" I asked.

"No," she said without smiling. She filled our glasses and asked us if we wanted another pitcher. We told her we had to leave but that we really liked her. She knew we were high.

When we left, I put my arm around Basille and told him how much I missed him when I was in Chicago.

"I never tell you that," I said. "I never say it enough."

"That's the drugs talking," Basille said.

★

Warren Puig was happy to see us. When we got to his loft he shook my hand and I introduced him to Basille. Meg wasn't there yet. He showed us around. I got a beer and he talked to me for a while about Chicago and New York and food.

"I hate that I can't eat pizza anymore," he said. "I'm on ulcer meds, stomach meds, pills for acid reflux. Two different anti-anxiety pills. Things quit working at my age. And I mean everything. It's all diseased. Sick. Gideon, did anyone ever tell you that you have a movie star face?"

The pain in my mouth was gone. When Meg arrived, she could tell we were fucked up. "What did you guys take?" she asked.

"They told us it was Ecstasy, but I think it might be Demerol or something."

I put my arms around her and told her how much I'd missed her. Puig's loft was huge and people were suddenly all around. He had an interesting looking tribal mask on top of the bookshelves that was red and brown striped, made of wood, with a sharp nose and a drooping mouth, a scowl. Pictures of abstract art hung on the walls. Photos on shelves of Puig with various people in cities and on beaches.

Meg gave me something that eventually made me feel strange and immobile. Everything felt infinitely colorful. The light was soft. I sat in a chair beside the window and watched everyone. There were colors and angles. Basille was standing across the room with a woman I couldn't seem to place. She gestured wildly with her hands while Basille nodded. People gathered around me, milled about. They breathed clouds of smoke, broke out in laughter. The woman kept gesturing, talking to Basille.

A black guy with dreads named Isaiah who played drums on upside-down buckets in front of a bar called Trees said his mother was a spiritualist. "She can connect with people's spirits," he told me. "You know someone who's passed on? She can hear them."

I listened to a girl hum something to a guy who kept blinking. He touched his hair, his nose, his chin. He blinked nervously as the girl hummed. They moved off to another part of the room. Conversations came all around me:

"I watched him fuck it up. Seriously. I watched the whole sick thing."

"She and I try to meditate for an hour every night. It isn't easy. My work stress fucks with me all night. I bring stress home with me. It's terrible. More wine?"

"Reported second quarter earnings of over a hundred million on the back of lower fees earned from a ten percent decline in assets under management."

"Have you seen Warren's wife?"

"Our son Phillip is twelve. He's brilliant. He eats swordfish."

"Narwhals hide behind dumpsters in Paseo. Spread the word."

"I'll give anyone twenty bucks right now if they can tell me the name of the lead singer of Bow Wow Wow."

I had the taste of battery acid in my mouth. Edie Kershaw, who said she was a folk singer from Austin, was talking about watching a mountain lion lick lichen in the dark. She sat with her hands between her knees and told me she was camping with her boyfriend when the mountain lion turned and looked at them. "Then it wandered off," she said. "A sort of miracle, really."

I stared at her. I found her beautiful. She asked if everything was okay then said she needed to speak to a friend across the room. I watched her walk away. A guy named Seth told me he lived in a crummy building near Elm. Another guy said he lived with two girls named Kristi and Janet.

"Like *Three's Company*," someone said.

"I think it was Chrissie? Was it Chrissie? Does anyone know?"

The girl with Seth said she'd lived in a halfway house on Myer Street for nine months. "They had a community bathroom on our floor," she said. "You had to have a key."

Margot Cox said she lived with her boyfriend in the same apartment where Lee Harvey Oswald lived before he shot Kennedy. "There are scratchings on the bedroom wall," she said.

"I read he was a somnambulist," someone said. "He would rearrange furniture in his sleep. Hang laundry on a line outside. Fill a sink with water and look for his reflection."

"The scratchings haunted me," Margot said. "Nights I couldn't sleep I would lie in bed, staring at them and wonder—what was he thinking?"

I stepped away to another part of the room. More conversations circled me:

"It's a carbuncle or something. I'm not sure what but it won't go away. I made another appointment with our doctor."

"If we're lucky we get her to bed by nine. She complains about noises in the hallway."

"You ever lash out at some jerkoff who's taking forever at the urinal?"

"He has a drifting eye. It's fucked. The eye practically hops. You're not sure which eye to look at when he's talking to you."

"Narwhals hide behind dumpsters in Paseo."

"When Phillip isn't doing homework or writing his science fiction novel, he spends nights playing chess online against a serial killer in prison."

"Annabella something. She wore a mohawk. Posed nude at age fourteen on the cover of their first album."

"Narwhals hide behind dumpsters. Spread the word."

"Twenty bucks right now to anyone who can name George Harrison's last album."

"Also the effect of an additional ten million shares outstanding from the firm's stock offering in December."

"He sat for hours at his cubicle doing nothing every day. Just sat there. Getting paid for it."

"Lower back problems. Hemorrhoids, impotence, a flare of psoriasis. All stress related, he says. He works overtime most weeks. Hates his job."

"Because, Phong, the algorithm can just be reverse engineered from the program."

"We wanted benzos from someone, but everyone was out. A guy under the freeway finally helped us out. I paid the guy and he exposed himself."

"And these are the company's most recent financial stability ratings?"

"Ask me Dylan. Ask me Hendrix. Anyone but The Who."

"Narwhals behind dumpsters."

Basille came over and told me someone had some pot, so we went into a bedroom and I watched him do a bong hit with Isaiah and another guy. I declined, needed to gather myself together. Then we were back in the main room, talking to Edie Kershaw and another girl. They were saying something about the recent decline of tattoo shops in Deep Ellum. Edie Kershaw raised her shirt and put her hand on the back of my head. She pulled my mouth to her navel. Her body felt warm on my mouth. Meg was sitting on the floor, talking to someone who looked dangerous and familiar. How was she able to interact, move, keep her language fluent and coherent? I sipped wine from a red plastic cup. At some point I was able to take necessary steps toward the balcony. Warren Puig stood beside a man in drag who smoked a long, thin cigarette. The man's wig was crooked and powdery. They both turned to me, and I stepped outside onto the balcony to vomit.

10

I woke at Meg's apartment. I couldn't remember leaving the party or the walk home. Basille was staring at the sky from the window. He saw I was awake and asked how I felt.

"I don't know," I said. "How long did I sleep?"

"Not long. You were freezing. I had to help you up the stairs."

The night was almost complete, the stillness visible, the light in the room dying. The sun would come up soon. I felt sick and drunk but compelled to do something. Meg had left Puig's place with someone Basille and I didn't know. He was tall and good-looking, possibly foreign, a roundish face. I watched Basille crouch down and put his ear to the floor.

"What are you doing?" I asked.

"You said there was a girl down there. A girl you met?"

"Yeah. You hear something?"

He was on his knees, head sideways, ear pressed against the hardwood floor. He looked at me. "I hear barking."

"Barking?"

He was listening but I couldn't hear anything.

"Barking?" I asked again.

"Barking. Definitely barking. Does she have a dog?"

"I don't know. I think she has a cat."

"Maybe someone else is there. Maybe someone with a dog."

"You're sure it's a dog?"

"Maybe it's the girl. Sounds like she's getting fucked." Basille was laughing now, drunk, crouched down on all fours with his ear pressed to the floor. "Barking," he kept saying.

I sat in the chair, drunk and immobile. Soon I was able to close my eyes, and when I opened them it was light. Meg stood beside me, touching my arm, saying my name. She was holding her cell phone. "Desi," she said. I sat up and took the phone from her.

"Sorry to wake you," said Desi.

"Hey."

"Your brother threw up on my couch. He also walked backwards. We tried to wake you but you wouldn't move. Basille was worried."

"What time is it?"

"Eleven. I'm off work at noon today. Want to get lunch?"

I squinted in the morning light. Meg was doing something in the kitchen. "I'm not sure," I said. "I need to see if I can get a ride from Meg."

"Text me and let me know," she said. "I work downtown on Houston Street. Meg knows where it is."

She gave me her number and I entered it into my phone. I went into the kitchen where Meg was standing, spreading jam on toast. She brought the knife to her mouth and licked it. "Basille's still asleep in my bed," she said. "So are you going to lunch with Desi?"

"Can I get a ride?"

"What are you looking for?" she asked. I was opening and closing cabinets. I found a bottle of aspirin, opened it and tipped three tablets into my hand. I poured a glass of water and swallowed them. Meg slinked away with her toast and coffee.

"Sawyer came by looking for you the other day," I said. "Mentioned something about Arwal."

"Down here they call it Possum Weed. You might like it."

She came over and put her arms around me, her way of apologizing. "Your face looks better," she said.

After I changed clothes she dropped me off at Desi's building. The receptionist at the front desk called Desi and buzzed me in. Desi met me at the door. She was dressed nice, different from before. She looked older, more professional.

"Hey," she said. "Come back and see where I work."

I followed her past all the supervisors' open offices, looking in as we passed each one. In the first, a woman talked on her cell and filed her nails. In the next office a man was putting a golf ball into a cocktail glass turned on its side. Then there was a man

51

lying on a couch, flipping through a car magazine. Next, a man wearing earphones played drums on his desk with two pencils. Then we came to the area of cubicles where Desi worked. She had her computer monitor decorated with a bunch of stickers and photos of her with her niece and friends from college.

"Everybody looks bored," I said.

"Nobody wants to be here," she said. She leaned in close and whispered. "You notice how fat everyone is? It's because we sit all day. Forty hours a week we sit in cubicles. Except when we go to court or have to transport a kid to placement."

"This isn't helping me get motivated."

An older overweight man sitting in the cubicle across from us was eating Chinese food hunched over at his desk and playing cards on the computer. Desi introduced us. He looked up and mumbled hello.

"Burt's a smart man," Desi said. "Ask him anything."

"How long have you worked here?" I asked.

"Over twenty goddamn years."

"Do you think I would like working in an office like this?"

"No."

Desi drove us to a Mexican restaurant downtown. The place smelled of fajitas and salsa. We sat in a booth and ordered. My head was feeling better, though a wave of fatigue came over me. I liked the sound of people all around us, the noise, the need to talk. I told Desi about the pill Meg gave me at Puig's party.

"I know," she said. "Basille told me. He said you were pretty fucked up."

"Do you have a dog?" I asked.

"A dog? No, just Sasha, my cat. Why?"

"No reason."

"Do you like dogs?" she asked.

"We had a dog when I was a kid. Part German Shepherd and Shar Pei. His name was Frito. You said Basille threw up on your couch last night?"

"He knocked on my door and woke me up. He was pretty drunk. Said he was your brother and that you guys heard noises."

"Noises?"

"I have night terrors," she said. "You probably heard me. I

sometimes wake up screaming. I've had it since I was little. Does that freak you out? You're looking at me all weird."

"It doesn't freak me out. Basille had them when we were kids. You actually scream?"

"Some nights."

"And then you invited Basille in?"

She studied me. "You're full of questions today, creepo. Did you know your brother is weird? He walked in backwards."

"He's been doing that since he was a kid. It's nothing."

She laughed. We ate fajitas and I told her about my mother going through a hard time. "I'm driving up to spend some time with her," I said.

"That's good of you," she said.

She drove us back to Deep Ellum Alley. She invited me inside her apartment and this time I followed her inside. In the kitchen she worked a corkscrew into a bottle of wine. I took off my coat and looked at her bookshelves and the framed pictures of her family on her coffee table. I heard a jackhammer beating the street somewhere down the block. Desi brought out the bottle and two glasses.

We sat on the couch and watched TV, some summer beach party show in Spanish. There was something wonderful about it, beautiful people dancing, a different time and season, a beach far away. We drank wine and then we were on the floor, our bodies pressed against each other. She got on top of me for a while. Then we sat up and watched more TV. She sat with her back against the couch. I put my head in her lap and felt her hand on my brow. We stayed like that, silent, for a long time.

11

The day darkened quickly. I felt like I hadn't seen much daylight. When I went upstairs to Meg's apartment nobody was there. I stood at the window. I could still hear the jackhammer.

I called Basille. "Where are you?"

"Home," he said. "Are you with the barking girl?"

"I was. A while ago."

"Apologize for me. I feel terrible. I never throw up unless I'm nervous. Somebody must've slipped me something. Weird crowd there."

"Might have been the mixture of the Ex and alcohol. When are you coming back? I want to go to Mom's tomorrow and stay a few days."

"I'll come tomorrow," he said. "I can drive you out there. Right now my head still hurts."

I went into the bathroom and took a Hydrocodone and my antibiotic. While I was brushing my teeth I heard a knock at the door, followed by the sound of someone entering. Two guys I didn't know let themselves in. The first guy had greased dark hair and wore yellow tinted glasses. The other guy was smaller, thinner, wearing a stocking cap and heavy coat. His bottom lip was scabbed.

"Meg around, bub?" the first guy said.

"Who are you?" I asked.

They were both looking around the room. "I'm Cal. This is Mick. Sorry to just barge in. Meg usually doesn't give a shit."

Mick was nervous and twitchy. He looked at me and nodded a hello.

"She's not here," I said. "I'm her brother."

"She'll be back soon?"

"No idea. I just got here myself. Have you tried her cell?"

He looked at me. "Last she told me her phone was broke and she was paying off bills before she got a new one. Did she get one?"

Meg must've given these guys some bullshit about losing her phone. "She hasn't told me anything," I said, "but I've only been around a couple of days. She's out most of the time."

The other guy, Mick, blew his nose in a wadded tissue. He examined the results and then stuffed it into his coat pocket. He seemed confused.

Cal squinted at me. "You think she's with Axel? I can't find him anywhere."

"I don't know Axel."

"Weird. She hasn't mentioned him?"

"No, but I've only been here two days. Do you know him?"

"Last we saw him he went berserk, told me to go fuck myself. All I got to say is, if your sister's with this guy you should be concerned, bub."

"Thanks for letting me know," I said.

"Alright, bub. We need to take off. No need to tell Meg we stopped by."

✶

Later Rick called and offered me the job at Reverb Brothers Guitars. I could start right away. "Come in tomorrow," he said.

I was happy and wanted to celebrate, but Meg was out and Basille was working and I couldn't get in touch with Sawyer. I made my way down the complicated streets, through Deep Ellum. It was freezing and I thought about going back to my mother's and staying for a few days and trying to spend time with Gene if it meant making her happy.

I wanted to stop in and see if Puig was home, but it was too late. I've always favored older males as friends. Meg once told me I yearned for a connection with a father figure. Basille, too. When we were kids, Basille and I used to take money from our mother's purse and walked past the railroad tracks to Poquita's, a Mexican restaurant, where we could buy cigarettes from a man named Don. He was an old guy, maybe a little slow, but nice to us. He lived in the apartment above Poquita's and let us come up to his place sometimes.

Besides selling us cigarettes, sometimes he let us watch videos of people fucking. He also collected unusual soda pop bottles, which Basille and I thought was cool. His place was full of shelved empty soda pop bottles.

I remember one day when Don was down with the flu. He answered the door in his robe, a blanket wrapped around his shoulders. "I'm sick," he told us. "Boys, please have a drink with me and help me feel better." Basille and I sat on his divan and watched TV while he watched us. He gave us each a bottle of soda pop. I drank Full Throttle Blue Demon. Basille drank Blood Orange. Don came over and sat between us. He showed us a certain way to drink from the bottle. On his TV we watched two people fuck for a long time. I felt tired. Wrapped in a blanket, Don cradled Basille's head to his chest. I leaned into them, too. We all must've looked sick or happy.

I went to work at Reverb Brothers Guitars. Rick started me out Windexing the glass cabinets and doors and windows. The rest of the time I stayed in the back room, inventorying equipment or restringing or straightening the necks on used guitars while Rick and his brother Vince made orders, gave lessons and handled business in the front.

Rick and Vince gave me a long lunch break and let me smoke in the back room while I worked. I went through the boxes when UPS arrived with a shipment of amps and pedals. I developed a rhythm to changing strings and tightening necks with an allen wrench. At the end of the day I vacuumed the carpet and took out the trash. It was six o'clock and dark outside before I knew it.

The first few days of work were like that. Rick and Vince told me I was doing good work and let me help out some with the register while they gave lessons. When I left the store at the end of the day I'd stop at a local bookstore on the corner and have coffee. I sat in a red chair for an hour or two and read before catching the bus back to Meg's place. I doodled and wrote down thoughts on napkins. The guy who owned the place was an older Native American man who walked with a limp and talked with a slur and let his golden retriever walk around the shop. I tried not to think about my mother's sickness or Meg or anything.

One night Meg wasn't home and I felt edgy, so I grabbed a bottled water from the fridge and went for a walk. It was freezing and I could see my breath in front of me. I decided to go see Puig. He understood loneliness. He was nothing like Gene.

I went upstairs to his loft and knocked. He opened the door

and looked surprised but pleased to see me. He'd been sitting at his desk, papers everywhere. He stood and greeted me, hugging me in a genuine and fatherly way, his shoulders curved forward. We sat on the divan and he poured me a glass of dark wine.

"I'm glad you're here," he said. "We didn't get a chance to talk enough the other night. How are you? You look cold."

"I was taking a walk," I said. "Looks like you're working. Should I come back later?"

"No, stay," he said. "Look at this mess. I'm trying to draw nudes from memory. How does that work? I'm supposed to be creative, a visionary. My wife's asleep in the next room." He motioned with his head to the door, which was closed.

He showed me some drawings and we talked. I checked my phone then texted Meg: *Where r u?*

Puig noticed and said, "Texting is a form of communication I can't understand."

"Beats talking."

"I could talk all night. You want some coffee or more wine?"

I texted Meg: *I'm at Puig's. Hope you're ok. C u at home soon.*

When I got back to the apartment, Meg was there, asleep on her side, curled up with the comforter pulled to her neck. She always slept quietly, barely moving. My jaw was still sore so I took my antibiotic and Hydrocodone. I thought it might help me fall asleep. I sat in the chair by the window, covering myself with an afghan. I finally fell asleep at some point, but not for very long. Meg was gone again when I woke.

I had a few days off work, so I rode with Basille in his beat up Honda to our mother's house. On the way we stopped at Walgreens so I could stock up on things I'd need for a few days: cigarettes, Tums, toothpaste. Basille stayed in the car with the heat blowing.

We drove out of downtown and headed northeast. "Remember when we met a midget once after the Chainsaw Kittens concert?" Basille asked. "A Mexican midget."

"He was smoking a cigar."

"He told us that taking peyote during sex can increase the spiritual experience."

"I don't remember that part."

"And that the African jumping spider is more likely to bite someone with gonorrhea."

"Shit, I don't remember that either."

"And that porcupine quills contain a sticky substance used to make beads but can cause extreme paranoia if swallowed."

"How do you remember all this?"

"I think of that guy sometimes when I'm driving alone," he said. "I don't know why. It takes my mind off thinking about redheads with freckles and pasty skin."

On the drive Basille told me that he'd recently done an interview with someone from *Dallas Arts* magazine about his life as a former winner of the Teen National Geography Bee. The lady who called wanted Basille to come to the office to do the interview but Basille told her he would only do it over the phone.

"They interview former child stars from Dallas," he said. "I don't know how I came up on that list. I told them I was no big deal, that nothing came of it. They didn't care, they still wanted to do the interview. I asked the woman who called if she had red hair."

We kept driving. Once we were on Route 1, the car started making noise. "What's that?" Basille said.

"Pull over," I said.

Basille pulled over to the side of the road. Thankfully there wasn't much traffic. We got out in the cold and saw that the back right tire was flat. I covered my head with my hoodie and blew on my hands. Basille opened the trunk and we got out the spare. I'd changed tires before—one thing Gene had taught me early on. Luckily Basille had tools. He got out the jack while I found a good size rock and placed it behind the good tire. I cranked the jack, and with a wrench tried to loosen the lugnuts but had trouble. They were on too tight. Basille tried and couldn't get any loosened either. Then he stood and, with his boot, kicked the wrench a few times, hard enough so that one loosened.

We stopped for a minute to blow on our hands. Soon we were able to loosen all the lugnuts and remove the tire. Then we put the spare on and tightened the lugnuts. It was the first flat I'd changed since I was a teenager.

It was late in the afternoon when we got to Red Owl. As soon as we pulled in to the drive, Gene came outside. He stood in his heavy coat, waving at us. I knew then that he had something planned. Anytime something needed to be done, he was eager to do it and volunteered me or Basille to help.

"We have a problem," he said, approaching me as I got out of the car. "Margaret Horn's dog died and we need to drive out to her brother's land and bury it."

"Right now?"

He looked at me. "Why are you wearing a woman's coat?"

"It's Meg's."

"Where's yours?"

"Long story," I said. "I left it in Chicago."

"I have an extra jacket in the hall closet if you want."

"I'm fine. I like this coat and Meg doesn't mind."

"It's a woman's coat."

"It's fine," I told him.

"This isn't Chicago. It looks ridiculous."

I started for Margaret Horn's house. Margaret Horn had lived next door to my mother and Gene since they'd moved out here.

She was a reclusive woman who never married and had lived with her elderly father until his death. She was the mother of twin boys who were born conjoined at the forehead. The boys survived the surgeries, and though their heads were slightly oblong and their foreheads large, they were able to live and function. Margaret homeschooled them. Sometimes you'd see her walking with them along Fulton Road, wiping drool from their mouths or helping them collect berries. Nobody knew who the father was. Gene once told me there were rumors that Margaret's father raped her, that he was the twins' father. The newspaper ran a story about the boys with their "before and after" surgery photos. She rarely went into town. The grocery store made special deliveries just for her. I'd never been inside her house and scarcely saw her or the boys.

"You'll at least need gloves," Gene said. "I have an extra pair inside." He looked at Basille. "Can you stay here with your mother? Someone needs to."

Basille agreed, and after I went inside and put on Gene's gloves and loaded Gene's pickup with two shovels from the garage, we went next door and got directions from Margaret Horn, a small, frail old woman who wore thick-lensed glasses. She sat in her recliner in front of the TV with a black poodle in her lap. Another dog, a bigger black lab that was lying on the rug in front of the divan, came over and sniffed at our feet. Being inside her house was odd. The living room smelled of dogs and had 1970s décor— old furniture and wallpaper. The carpet was a fading lime green. There were chewed dog toys and old tennis balls on the floor.

"Thank you, boys," she said weakly. "Ricardo's out on the back patio." She told us the dog died of old age. "He was such a good dog," she went on. She kept thanking us for burying him for her. I felt sorry for her. Then we went out to the covered patio. We'd brought an old blanket along to wrap him with.

The covered patio was a mess. The dogs had chewed up the legs of a small table and ripped the stuffing from an old chair. There were paw marks on the window and all over the screen door that led outside. Ricardo, the dog that had died, wasn't too big, maybe thirty or forty pounds. He was white, long-legged with brown spots. He was lying on his side, eyes open, tongue protruding from his mouth.

"Let's get the blanket under him," Gene said. We knelt down and wrapped him in the blanket. I carried Ricardo around the house to the pickup and Gene went to get directions to her brother's farm. While I waited for Gene I got the bottle of Hydrocodone from the pocket of Meg's coat, opened it and swallowed a pill. I felt my jaw, which was much better.

We took Route 1, which followed a field out of town until we turned onto a gravel road. Gene drove slowly then, the gravel snapping under the tires. We came to a wooded area and saw Mildred Thorn's brother's house and a barn. Gene pulled in and we got out.

"Margaret's brother isn't here?" I asked.

"Out of town," Gene said. "She said we should bury him just past the barn over there. We should be able to see where other dogs are buried. I'll get the shovels if you carry the dog."

I made sure the blanket was wrapped around him, then lifted him from the truck. I carried Ricardo while Gene walked ahead of me. As we walked I could see Ricardo's head protruding out of the blanket, the exposed tongue, open eyes. We went around the barn to the area near the trees where the other dogs were buried. There were three metal crosses in the ground.

I set the dog down on the ground and we started digging. The ground was hard from the recent freeze. The Hydrocodone made me weak. As I dug I noticed a donkey standing behind Gene, staring at us. Gene turned around and raised his shovel, yelling at it to go away. The donkey jerked and stepped back. Gene jabbed at it with the shovel. Finally the donkey turned and took a few steps. "Goddamned animal," he said.

We finished digging a hole deep enough to hold Ricardo. We unwrapped the blanket and Gene helped me lift the dog into the grave. Then we filled the grave and packed it down. Gene took a minute to catch his breath. We were both cold.

"I guess Margaret's brother will weld a cross," he said.

As we walked back the donkey approached us again. Gene jabbed toward it with the shovel until it backed away. "Go away," he said. "Move it."

The drive back was quiet. I thought about how I would spend time with Gene for the next few days. It occurred to me how old he looked, how morose he'd become. When we got back, we noticed Basille's car was gone. "I told that boy to stay here until we got back," he said. "You go inside and check on your mother. I'll check on Margaret."

I found my mother sitting in the living room, reading the paper. I was happy to see her out of the bedroom. A cigarette burned in the ashtray beside her. She looked up at me briefly, then looked back at the paper.

"Where's Basille?" I asked.

"He was called in to work."

"At the frame shop?"

"No. The bar needs him to play tonight."

She sat with her back to the window, flipping through the paper. There were loose pieces of paper from a scratch pad all around her with numbers scribbled on them.

"What's all this?" I asked.

"Gene was working on the budget earlier. He has to do it every few months."

Dust motes floated in a slant of light from the window. My mother folded the newspaper and set it beside her on the divan. She looked at me and tried to smile. I could feel the pressing intensity in the room, the need for something more.

"Think I'll make some coffee," I said. "You want some?"

"No," she said. "Thanks."

I went into the kitchen and brewed a pot. Gene came back in and made us tomato soup. We ate in the kitchen while my mother went back to bed. I crumbled a fistful of Saltines into my bowl and ate, head down. Gene kept asking me what my plans were.

"I don't know," I said. "I don't know."

At one time he would've argued with me, but now he sounded more concerned than angry. "Your mother," he said. "She'll be okay."

I wasn't sure I believed him. I looked up, but he kept eating his soup. He ate it the same way I'd been eating mine, head down.

-14-

The rural setting of Red Owl made Gene paranoid. He used to stand outside at night and listen for animal noises he thought were coming from the woods. He'd seen mountain lions roaming around in the woods off Fulton Road some nights. He told us they attacked humans. There were coyotes who threatened neighbors' chickens and baby quail. He also worried about burglars and vandals. Once, there were some teenagers who stopped down on Fulton Road late one night. They were drinking and yelling and making a lot of noise. Gene called the cops then went outside and fired a shotgun in the sky to scare them away.

Gene made omelets for supper. My mother wasn't hungry so Gene and I sat by ourselves at the table in the kitchen and ate. He wasn't interested in talking much. I found him different than he used to be—serious, irritable, less interesting. When I was younger he always wanted to go somewhere, fishing or on hunting trips, camping, driving to lakes. Or he liked to play cards with friends.

After we ate we joined my mother in the living room. I was glad to see her out of the bedroom, out of bed, even if she was still in her bathrobe. She was smoking and watching The Weather Channel. An anchor in Buffalo was describing blizzard conditions. He stood at the airport, wearing a hooded heavy coat and gloves, holding a microphone to his face. The snow blew sideways in a strong wind. I thought surely this man must hate his job. He pointed to the airport behind him and mentioned flight delays. Gusts of wind created static in his microphone.

Gene put in a disc he'd converted from an old VCR tape and then sat back down on the sofa and put his arm around my mother. She sat smoking, an ashtray in her lap.

We watched ourselves from many years ago. Meg and I when

we were little, pretending to be newscasters. I sat in the recliner and watched. There we were, Meg and I, sitting at the kitchen table, ages nine and twelve. There we were, talking about the news of the world: airplane crashes and wildfires sweeping the western plains, people dying, animals being rescued from rivers by helicopters, killer sharks, ice sculptures in Antarctica, poisonous rattlesnakes and bees swarming in Texas and Oklahoma. I watched the younger version of myself reading from a piece of notebook paper. I observed Meg's seriousness, her youthfulness, the expressions of horror as she read these fictional news stories. The picture was poor quality, copied from an old VCR tape with bad tracking. I tried to find humor in watching it—surely this was what Gene and my mother expected—but they weren't laughing either. Soon I found myself watching them as they watched the video, studying it as if seeing us for the first time, never smiling or commenting on anything.

The video showed me sitting at the piano, staring at sheet music. Then Basille at age six, wearing a cowboy hat and playing a toy trumpet. Then there was a Christmas from a few years ago. The video showed all of us sitting in this very room, watching ourselves on TV. Every year on Christmas we watched ourselves opening gifts from previous Christmases.

"I don't remember this," my mother said.

"It was what, seven or eight years ago?" Gene asked.

"Fifteen at least," I said. "Look how young Basille is."

They studied the video. Our mother took a drag of her cigarette and tapped it into the ashtray on her lap. We watched footage of her, packing for a gambling trip to Tunica. She was sitting in their hotel room at the El Dorado, counting money, drinking a vodka on the rocks. Waving to the camera at the pool, sitting under an umbrella in the sun. Then she held up a T-shirt with the words *Reno, Nevada* on it.

"This is when we stayed at the El Dorado Motel in Reno," Gene said. "Next door to a Mexican restaurant with outdoor seating. One night I ate a cornmeal crusted chile relleno with roasted eggplant and sweet red pepper sauce that gave me a terrible case of heartburn. Terrible."

I checked my cell phone. Nobody had texted.

"One thing about these road trips that I always appreciated was that your mother and I were able to talk," Gene said.

The TV showed my mother in a dress, looking at herself in a hotel mirror. She picked up a cigarette and waved the camera away. "This was when we went to see Keith Jarrett in concert." He looked at my mother.

"That's right," she said. "Keith Jarrett understands sin and redemption."

15

Gene wanted to go to the market for groceries. "Gideon, you can come with me," he said. "The time together will be good."

I was sure this was just an attempt to please my mother. I went into my old bedroom and put on Meg's coat. I took a Hydrocodone from the pocket and popped it in my mouth. When I went back into the living room, Gene was pulling on his boots. "Are you wearing that coat again?" he asked. I stood there looking at him. His knees cracked as he stood. My mother looked at Gene. "It looks fine on him," she said.

It was a ten-minute drive to the market. We drove down Fulton Road and turned onto Highway 6, Gene observing the speed limit. At the market he pushed a cart and so did I. I reviewed the list he gave me and we went down different aisles. On the way back we stopped at a bar called Mill's Tavern, a small joint near the market, so Gene could have a drink.

Inside we sat on redwood barstools next to a couple of old guys I didn't know. I ordered a beer and Gene ordered a bourbon. I'd never been inside Mill's Tavern, but I'd heard stories about the original owner, Russell Mill, an old Korean War veteran who walked with a bad limp and in his spare time bred and sold wolf-dog pups until so many of them ended up in the shelter that animal control came down hard on him. The dogs were late-night howlers and incessant diggers and too skittish for most owners. When Russell Mill died, his son took over the bar. I'd never met him, but Gene once told me that Russ Jr. held big stakes illegal poker games in a room upstairs from the bar. Then everybody started going out to the Indian casino when it opened up thirty miles north. Mill's Tavern was a shabby old saloon with a plank floor, dark wood paneling. An old jukebox played Johnny Cash: *Early one mornin' while makin' the rounds, I took a shot of cocaine and*

I shot my woman down. "Buddy of mine from Oklahoma played this song at his wedding," the guy sitting next to Gene said. The bartender and the other guy laughed.

"Doesn't quite strike me as a wedding song," the bartender said.

I took a drink of my beer and looked at my reflection in the mirror behind the bottles. I looked tired and weak.

"We should use these next couple of days to figure out what to do about Meg," Gene said.

"What are you worried about?"

"Her shooting dope and hanging around bad people."

"She is gone a lot," I said. "But I'm not too worried."

"We think she's doing dope again."

I took a drink and shrugged. Gene always overreacted. I was used to listening to his worries.

"She borrows money," he said. "Disappears for long periods of time and we don't hear from her.

I took a swig of beer.

"It's serious, Gideon."

"You think this is what caused Mom's breakdown?"

He turned away and stared at the counter, shaking his head. "Your mother has all sorts of issues she's dealing with," he said. "You don't want to know. One thing that would make her feel better is to not worry about Meg. And for you and I to get along." He sipped his bourbon. "I think we should pay this guy Axel a visit. What do you know about him?"

"Nothing. She won't tell me anything."

"I went through her cell phone a while back and tried to find his address," he said. "No luck. This guy is bad news. I can feel it."

Gene was right. We needed to talk to Axel and see if he was bad for Meg.

Otis Gulch, a hunting friend of Gene's, came over and said hello. He was by himself. He looked so old I almost didn't recognize him. Before he'd retired he owned a foundry up north in Michigan. He told me the story numerous times, how he worked his way up from shop foreman to plant manager. Some years later he bought out a foundry and introduced a number of innovations to the plumbing industry. Now that he was retired he took to hanging out in the bar and deer hunting with Gene. He took a liking to me, I think, because I talked motorcycles with him. He and his wife both owned Harleys and took weekend rides when I was younger.

"Who the hell is this?" he asked Gene, grabbing my arm playfully.

"Nice to see you Otis," I said. "Still riding a Harley?"

"Sold it last year. After Junior's wreck."

"Good old Junior," Gene said.

I didn't know who they were talking about but gathered someone had died in a motorcycle crash. Otis's breath was like a sewer in my face. You could see in him the years of hard work and booze. He took a drink of his beer and gave me a pat on the shoulder.

"Good old Junior," he said. "He was a good old boy. Died too young."

Gene agreed. "Reminds me of an old song. Isn't there an old country song about a dog or boy named Junior?"

"I reckon there probably is but I can't think," Otis said, reflecting.

Gene sipped his drink. "Junior was a hard worker."

"Yep."

"A goddamned saint."

There was a slow, sad country song playing on the jukebox, and for a moment neither of them said anything.

On the drive back a light frost sprinkled the windshield. I found myself struggling to stay awake, my eyes focusing on the grooves of the road in the headlights. The windshield wipers squeaked. Driving at night in the country was spooky, darkness all around us. A cold silent night, freezing outside, sleet pelting the windshield. I fought to keep my eyes open.

Suddenly an animal with glowing eyes appeared in the headlights. Gene slammed hard on the brakes and the animal bound away into the darkness. We were both quiet for a moment, stunned by the sudden shock. Maybe it was because we had been drinking, or that it was late and dark and wet outside.

When we got back to the house Gene wanted to sit up and talk. My mother was in bed. Gene poured himself a bourbon on ice and sat in a chair beside me in the back den. We sat in an awkward silence. I just wanted to sleep. I was doing this for my mother; we both were. I watched him take a drink and set the glass on the coffee table between us. I told myself I wouldn't fight with him. I tried to talk about my mother's breakdown.

"She just likes to keep to herself in our bedroom," he said. "She's developing little quirks. I don't understand them all. Maybe that's where Basille gets them from."

"Quirks?"

"Like the way Basille walks in and out of rooms backwards. Hers aren't that extreme though. Like every night she watches old movies with the sound muted. Sound's not important. She says it gives her a sense of peace and comfort, like when she was young. The flicker of light from the TV puts her at ease."

"What else?"

"She smokes in bed, alone."

"She's always done that."

He thought about this. "You're probably right."

I wondered if Gene felt guilty in some way for her overdose. I wanted to change the subject but Gene didn't ask me any questions. We sat a while, looking out the large window in front of us. We saw trees and darkness outside. Soon Gene finished his drink and stood from the chair. "I'm going to bed," he said, walking to the kitchen. He turned off the lamp on his way.

In the hall I saw my mother in the bathroom, barefoot, in her nightgown, washing her face. She was leaning over the basin and didn't hear me. I started to tell her goodnight but decided against it.

Late in the night Gene woke me from a deep sleep. By the digital clock it was a quarter to three.

"Get dressed," he whispered. "It's about Meg. I need you to come with me."

I pulled on some clothes and hurried into the kitchen where I thought Gene was, but he wasn't in the house. Out the front window I saw him walking with a shotgun toward the woods across Fulton Road. I put on Meg's coat and went out the front door, hurrying to catch up with him.

When I caught up he turned to me. "What the hell's wrong with you?" He put a finger to his lips for me to be quiet. "Follow me," he said.

The ground was hard and frozen and my feet were hurting. We walked down a path and crossed a creek. Gene stopped walking and motioned for me to be quiet. He looked around in the dark. I couldn't hear anything and told him so.

"I heard voices earlier," he said. "I got up and turned on the porch light and saw something run into the woods. Something dark, shadowy."

"What does this have to do with Meg?" I asked.

"People know where we live. Her people. Wise up, Gideon." He stopped talking and looked around.

"Could've been a deer or bobcat," I said. "Maybe some kids from town or something."

"I don't think so," he said. "They got away for tonight, but at least they know I'm on to them."

We walked back to the house, and for the rest of the night I had trouble falling asleep.

Late in the morning when I woke up, Gene was in town at his shop. My mother poured a cup of coffee in the kitchen and told me good morning.

"How you feeling?" I asked.

"I'm OK," she said. She sipped her coffee and looked at me through a long strand of gray hair that hung in her face. I'm not sure if it was the lighting or her unkempt hair, but for the first time I saw my mother as an aged woman. She held her coffee cup with both hands and walked back toward her bedroom.

I was thankful to sit alone and drink coffee in the living room. I looked out the window and saw patches of ice that glistened in the sun. It was cold outside, but the sun was shining.

I called Meg and asked if she was up.

"I'm sick," she said. "I've been throwing up all night. Be glad you're not here."

"I think you should come tomorrow."

"I need to get better so I can go out and look for a job. How are things there?"

"Not too bad," I said. "Are you sure you're okay?"

71

"I have company."

"Who?"

"A couple of friends," she said.

"Do I know them?

"Axel and Shawn. You don't know them. Don't worry. I'll talk to you later."

"If you feel better come out here, OK?"

"We'll see, Gideon."

I went to check on our mother. I opened the door and peeked into her bedroom, but she was back asleep, so I watched TV a while until Gene came home. I told him Meg was sick.

"She's always sick," he said.

I needed to get out of the house. I went out back to the old shed and pulled the chain for the light bulb. There was all sorts of junk in there. A small engine, old cords, rags, metal, boards, a small box of nuts and bolts. One time Gene tried to teach me how to rebuild a motorcycle engine. I was fourteen, fifteen. We stood in the shop one summer night with the light on. Outside it was getting dark and humid, bugs everywhere—the way summer nights are in Texas. It was an old 250cc Honda motorcycle with a bad clutch that Basille and I used to ride. Gene took the clutch apart and explained the parts, panels and plates, the importance of heat and friction. He handed me parts while he loosened and tightened things. He talked like a man bored with his work, but at least seemed eager to teach me. He wanted me to be interested in something.

When I came back inside later, my mother was sitting at the kitchen table reading a recipe book. She didn't look up when I walked in.

"Are you cooking something?" I asked.

Her gray hair was astray. She hooked a strand of hair behind her ear and kept reading. I wasn't sure if she was ignoring me or if she was concentrating hard. She was like that. You could sit and talk to her if she was reading or watching TV and after five minutes she wouldn't know a word you said.

I sat across from her at the table. "What are you doing still up?"

"I don't sleep well anymore," she said. "I slept for a while but a bad dream woke me up." She dog-eared the page and closed the book. She looked past me. Her face was pale and tired looking. "I have strange dreams." She stood from the table and set the book on the counter. She said she was going back to bed and touched my shoulder as she walked past.

I sat at the table for a while, staring at the digital clock on the oven. It was late. I texted Meg and asked how she was feeling. She didn't reply.

16

Gene was always an early riser. No matter how early I got up, he was already making coffee in the kitchen or reading the paper at the table. He used to always make snide remarks about everyone sleeping later than him. Today he was up early as usual. He sat at the kitchen table, eating breakfast and reading the paper.

"Sleep well?" he said. "I didn't."

I poured a cup of coffee and sat across from him. "I guess."

He chewed with a mouth full of lettuce and egg. "Bought me a tree stand in Dallas last week and could use some help putting it up."

"Tree stand?"

"For deer hunting. There's only a few weeks left of deer season. Why don't you come with me?"

"Sure."

We took his pickup to a woodsy area where he always hunted. During the drive he told me that last Thanksgiving he and his buddy had found the perfect spot. "There's a backbone of a ridge out here," he said. "You'll see."

As a teenager I'd gone deer hunting with him once but didn't like it. Basille didn't like it either. Gene always had his hunting friends and I was just glad when he got out of the house. I think he was also glad to get away from us. He always acted disappointed that we never wanted to go, but never felt guilty about going off and doing his own thing.

We pulled off the road and parked in the grass. I carried the stand for him while he walked ahead. The area wasn't too far. Gene had already installed the steps onto the tree before the last winter storm hit. While he put on his climbing belt, he told me the tree was downwind and away from a deer's line of sight. "There's a natural funnel in the wind," he said. "Your scent will drift over the deer."

74

He scaled up the tree with the stand. In a few minutes he was already ten feet up. He tied a rope from the hip of his harness to the stand's upright part. He did it like it was routine. This was a man who'd spent his entire life hunting deer and dove and quail. A man who grew up as poor as me but knew so much more about these things. I'd never had an interest in hunting, only fishing.

I watched him attach the stand, pushing the platform up and cinching the strap. He pulled it tight, then lowered the platform and pulled down on the stand to seat it.

"How's it going?" I called out, looking up at him.

He gave me a nod. He positioned himself, gripped the stand and sat down. He looked around, then down at me. "This'll work," he said. "Yes sir."

We drove back in a light rain. Gene went to bed early and I couldn't sleep. I went into the living room and turned on the TV. Nothing was on. I flipped through Gene's collection of *The Tonight Show* episodes starring Johnny Carson. He had every season, every episode. Johnny on every cover. Johnny as a young man, thin, in suit and tie. An older Johnny with white hair. I put in a few of the DVDs and fast-forwarded through them. It was strange. They were a distant form of life from another land, a time I barely recalled, Johnny of the seventies and eighties. I remembered being a young boy and staying up late some nights, watching the show with my mother and Gene.

For an hour or so I sat in a recliner and smoked, watching snippets of opening monologues. What was it about this man that Gene and my mother were so drawn to? I saw Johnny as an enigma, a strange object of Gene's obsession, a man of wit and sarcasm. Johnny, the king of late night television. A man of slapstick humor, dressed in drag and doubled-over in laughter. I fast-forwarded through the interviews, the musicians, the weird jugglers and stand-up comedians. I watched Johnny's skits. Johnny getting a pie in the face in fast-motion, Johnny smoking an exploding cigar, Johnny in swim trunks, splashing around in a tank of water.

While the DVD was playing I tried to call Meg but got her voicemail. I texted her: *What's going on? Think u can come pick me up in a few days?* Then I flipped through old VHS tapes and DVDs. I put in a DVD labeled "Gideon's B-Day" and watched myself as a teenager, maybe fourteen or fifteen, looking bored, burned out, wasted. I was sitting on the couch while Meg filmed me. I was wearing sunglasses, waving her away. Meg was trying to get me to laugh. Nobody else was around. Meg kept laughing and saying, "Hello, hello? What do you want me to do? What do you want, Gideon? What do you want me to do?"

I turned it off. A replay of the local news was on. A 23-year-old woman had been murdered in south Dallas. The reporter said the woman had been seen just days earlier by family members. She had no criminal history and was an innocent victim. The man arrested for her murder was part of a drug and human trafficking ring in Dallas. The police detective interviewed said the woman was a victim of opportunity, murdered in front of two other women involved in the ring.

It rained all night and I slept a restless sleep. That night I had a dream I was walking home through the field of tall grass past Fulton Road. I was twelve, thirteen. Someone was following me. When I turned around to look, he crouched down so I couldn't see him. It was someone who was after me. I ran hard through the grass, trying to hurry home. I was afraid the man knew I'd seen him. I was afraid something bad would happen.

The next day I overheard our mother talking to Meg on the phone. I was about to enter her bedroom but then stopped when I heard her voice. She was going on about how thoughtless and inconsiderate Meg was toward everyone.

"I'm not telling you to come out here," she said. "I'm not sitting here feeling sorry for myself or for anyone else for that matter. I've already told you how I feel about it. It's your decision and it hurts my feelings."

Gene came in and I backed away from the door. He noticed me standing there and asked what I was doing.

"Mom's on the phone and I didn't want to bother her," I said.

"Is she upset? Who's she talking to?"

"I don't know."

I stepped outside to the backyard and smoked a cigarette. I didn't want to have to listen to Gene. My main frustration with him was that he never thought I was tough enough to take care of myself. Once, when I was fourteen, I got into a fight after school with a boy who hit me in the mouth and bloodied my lip. I'd managed to hit the kid a few times, but he got the better of me. Gene tried to show me some boxing moves, but I wasn't interested. A few years later he wanted me to take a class in shooting a rifle at a place called Holt's. He told me the Holt Defensive Pistol and Rifle Training class focused on the three primary areas: *marksmanship* (hitting the target), *manipulation* (handling the weapon) and *mindset* (100% concentration, 100% of the time). The class instructor evidently had a background in law enforcement and tactical operations. He taught the importance of timing and concentration.

Gene spent a great deal of time trying to get me interested in this class. The instructor, he told me, emphasized single and multiple threats, shooting on the move, tactical loading and reloading. He assured me that the class always stressed safety. On the shooting range, people wore goggles and ear protection, as they fired round after round of ammunition. "Put effective rounds on target," Gene said. "Show marksmanship. Mindset. Aim."

Around that time I had a jarring dream about getting shot in the stomach and finding myself in a hospital bed and being awakened, oddly enough, by Mark David Chapman. I couldn't remember Chapman's name but knew him as the man who shot John Lennon. Chapman leaned in close with his creepy grin behind tinted glasses, his face weirdly magnified, like the reflection of a face in a spoon. There followed the sound of police sirens. Dogs barking. At some point I became aware that Meg was in the bed beside me, getting fucked by a man wearing a security guard uniform. Moaning in pain. The rest is blurry. I woke feeling ashamed, sprawled in a tangle of sheets, a slant of light coming from between the curtains. I wrote the dream down in my journal but never shared it with anyone, not even Basille.

On the day I told Gene I wouldn't take the class, he later came into my bedroom and said he needed my help right away in the living room. He had purchased a new VCR. He stood looking down at it, still packaged in plastic bubble wrap. A long band of yellow light beamed through the window and spread against the carpet. Lots of little white styrofoam balls were scattered on the floor.

He stroked his chin and made little clicking noises with his tongue. "We need to pull the television away from the wall so we can see what the hell we're doing. Then we'll hook up the VCR. This will give us some entertainment."

"Why?" I asked.

"Because it needs to be done." Gene said this loud enough while looking toward the hallway, for my mother to hear from the next room. "There are movies on cable. Good movies. Mystery. Music. Horror. The mordant humor."

"Right."

"The special effects," he said. "The guns. The intense moments of cruel and pointless drama. The explosions." He produced a handkerchief from his pocket and rubbed at his face and neck. "Now why don't you help me move this cocksucker." He got down on one knee beside the TV.

I wiped my nose with a tissue and then looked at Gene.

"Good mother of Christ, just throw that thing away," he said.

I hurried into the kitchen and tossed it in the wastebasket, then returned to help. The TV was an old RCA model with a mahogany cabinet and knobs beside the screen. It was heavy enough that Gene grunted while we slid the television on the carpet away from the wall so that it was turned sideways. Then I opened the plastic bubble wrap and took the VCR instructions out.

At that moment my mother walked over to the window. She lit a cigarette and looked out through the curtains at the lawn in the backyard, where Meg was sitting in the sun. At that time Meg was heavy into music and spent a lot of time outdoors with a notebook, killing whole afternoons trying to parse out the lyrics to Siouxsie and the Banshees songs.

Gene cracked his knuckles. "Read to me what the instructions say about basic operation," he said.

"*Instrucciones simplificadas. Oprimir...para...desconectar...*"

"Hold it right there. Do you or do you not know how to read a basic instruction manual?"

I handed him the instructions and he read them to himself. "Ah," he said.

I pressed on a small styrofoam ball with my foot.

"It's all just input and output," he said. "Male and Female. There's an illustration drawn up here." He went on to explain that the VHF/UHF OUT plug on the VCR should be connected to the VHF/UHF IN plug on the television, provided we had a two-wire monitor cable, which we did, since Gene had the foresight to buy one at Radio Shack on his way home from work. He sat on the couch and crossed his legs. I noticed one sock was navy blue and the other was black.

"What you can do since you're just standing around," he said, "is go in the bedroom and get the two-wire cable I bought. It'll be on my bed in the Radio Shack sack."

In ten minutes Gene had the VCR hooked up to the TV. He picked up the remote control and turned both the TV and VCR on. He was sipping his drink and aiming the remote control at the VCR, changing channels.

"Look at that," he said. "Piece of cake."

On TV was an old black-and-white comedy skit of Milton Berle and Bob Hope dressed as women. The audience laughed and applauded as the two men smiled dumbly at each other. Gene laughed long and hard.

Something about that laugh. I remember thinking I was like a dog waiting for his command.

"You can leave now," he said.

This, I remember, was when I first began to hate him.

17

I sent Meg a text telling her I was worried about our mother. She was asleep in a drift of blankets and hadn't left the bedroom. I didn't want to wake her. Gene had left to go hunting. Meg texted me back: *She's fine.* The text made me mad. Bored, I climbed up into the attic and found boxes of old photo albums, old drawings and newspaper clippings. It was here I found the notebook containing Meg's stories and plays she'd written when we were younger. I used to dress up and perform in her bedroom, with Basille as our only audience. As I flipped through it, I realized there was a thread of destruction in all the stories. The notebook, as I now saw it, contained the writings of a very sad girl, and I paraphrase here to help me gain an understanding of my sister:

1. "Volmk the Invisible Boy": A short, one act play about a girl named Anabella who is visited by an invisible and gentle boy named Volmk, whom she falls in love with. The only lines of dialogue are Annabella's. At the end she dies heartbroken when she is placed in a mental hospital.

2. "Flumley Learns to Speak": Another short, one act play, this one about a farm girl named Mary and her donkey named Flumley. One afternoon, while feeding Flumley from her hands, the donkey says her name. From there, she teaches him the alphabet, nursery rhymes and lullabies, which they sing together every morning for many years until they are both old and frail. Mary dies staring at a rainbow after a morning rain, and Flumley lies down to die beside her.

3. "Gepetto Goes to Greece": A short story about Gepetto traveling by boat to Greece to rescue Pinocchio, who has been kidnapped by the wicked old man who captured the donkey boys at Pleasure Island. When Gepetto arrives in Greece, he

is robbed and beaten by a drunken ship merchant and ends up a beggar. The story ends several years later when a much older and dirtier Pinocchio is walking down a dark alley. Not recognizing his father, he spits on him as he walks by.

4. "The Sad Tale of a Young Marionette": A short story about a new marionette named Sophia who is bought by a candy store owner and placed on a shelf along with other marionettes for decoration in the store. Some nights after the store is closed, the owner's son sneaks in and arranges the marionettes in various lewd sexual positions.

5. An unfinished story about a boy who is lulled to sleep by an old woman singing. While the boy is sleeping, the old woman begins exploring his body.

6. "The Nunkheads": An unfinished story about two hideous dwarves who fall in love with the same woman, who has no legs.

7. An unfinished story about a girl who collects strange objects and hides them under her bed.

8. An unfinished story about a set of twins conjoined at the forehead.

Meg was a prolific writer whose inspiration came from our neighbor down the road, Aviva Crump, an aging widow whose husband left her in the early eighties to become a missionary in Liberia. She used to sit outside in a broad-brimmed khaki hat and let Meg and Basille and I watch her paint with acrylics and oils on canvas. Her paintings were my first introduction to art. In a dusty room in her house she kept her large canvases among books and old toys and boxes full of photographs from her childhood. She dipped live tadpoles and goldfish into bright colors and let them squirm around on the canvas, creating abstract images.

I grew to like Aviva Crump. Meg liked her even more. We played marbles on her back patio. They were marbles she'd bought at the Tsa La Gi Cherokee Trading Post up in Tahlequah, eastern Oklahoma. She said they were used for other things, magical things, to help inspire her work. Meg spent more time with Aviva Crump after I grew bored with it all.

In the attic with her stories, I found one of Meg's old cassette tapes labeled: "Me and G and C." I took it downstairs to the garage and played it in the old cassette player. What I heard was Meg with two other people: another girl and a man, neither voices of which I recognized.

A light snow was falling outside. I put on Meg's coat and left the house for a while. Down the road was a small pond where I went fishing as a kid. In the winter we used to go down there when the ice was forming on the trees. We'd hang on the branches and let the icicles drop into the dark water. Meg called this area the Ice World and said it came alive in winter. One winter an ice storm hit and Meg and Basille and I walked down there with a boy from the neighborhood named Scotty. We were jumping and hanging on the branches and watching ice fall when Scotty slipped on the ice and busted his mouth. His lip was bloody and he was yelling in pain. We were maybe nine or ten at the time. We helped him up and walked him home. His mother told us we should've been more careful. "Scotty's only eight," she said. "You kids are too big to be playing with him. Now go on home."

I thought about that day as I walked down to the pond. The branches hung low over earth and pond. There wasn't a lot of ice, but patches of snow were on the ground and around the trees. The wind was calm by the water. I realized I was out of cigarettes and left, heading down Fulton Road. I walked down to the little store on the corner of Fulton and Wyatt. The woman who rang me up was an older woman with a kind of veiled, dreamy pout. She had a chiseled chin and cheekbones, gray-blonde hair. I'd never seen her before. On my way out I saw Antonio Perez, who lived in a small house a few miles from us. Antonio's oldest son Edgar was in school with me, so I got to know Antonio. He limped over to me and put his hand on my shoulder. "How are you, my friend?" he said.

"Fine, just visiting my mom. How is Edgar?"

"Working out in Arizona, driving a truck. Life for him is good right now. But plumbing problems for me tonight. And my grandson's sick. I need cough medicine and a plumber."

"I might be able to help with the plumbing."

"The faucet makes a noise and spits. I don't know what to do. I can't afford a plumber."

"I can have a look," I said. Gene had taught me some things about plumbing when I was younger. After Antonio bought red peppers and cough medicine inside, I rode with him in his pickup to his house. The neighborhood was quiet. The other houses had cars parked in yards. They were wood-frame houses with chipped paint. Antonio's house was filled with people—relatives, I assumed. There were seven or eight kids playing on the floor and watching TV. There were two other men who smiled and nodded as I walked in. Antonio's wife and another woman were watching something on TV, but from all the noise the kids were making I don't know how they were able to hear anything.

"Cough medicine and red peppers," Antonio said, handing the bag to his wife. "And I brought the miracle man."

Everyone said hello as I followed Antonio into the kitchen. He turned on the water. The faucet coughed, then made a gurgling noise. Water burst from the spigot.

"I have tools," Antonio said.

"Where's the valve? We just need a screwdriver and pliers."

We went downstairs to the cellar. Pipes were vibrating. We found the valve next to a box meter. I turned the valve to shut off the water. There was corrosion between the gear teeth of the pliers, so I hit it a couple of times against the floor.

"Good thinking," Antonio said.

Back upstairs I disassembled the cold water handle. With the screwdriver I chipped at the plaster, then put everything back together again. Antonio went downstairs and turned the water back on.

"Bingo," I yelled, turning the faucet on and off.

Antonio was overjoyed. "That easy?"

"I hope so."

"You saved me money," he said, inviting me to stay for coffee and dessert. "Rosa made pie." He took plates from the cupboard and cut us both a piece of banana pie. We sat in the kitchen and he talked about his job

"I just got a job at a guitar shop in Dallas," I said.

"That's good," he said. "I used to work in Dallas. You do okay there, make decent pay. I worked with troubled kids in a residential treatment center. Forty hours a week I tried to help kids who had addictions. When people asked what I did, I just told them I worked with kids. It could've been worse. I could've been typing or filing or logging numbers into a computer or something."

"That doesn't sound too bad."

We talked for a while longer in the kitchen. On the way out, in the living room, Antonio's son Freddie stood by the fish aquarium, staring into the glass. I stopped and knelt down next to him. The filtering system was bubbling, but I couldn't see any fish. I tapped the glass. "Anything in there?"

"He's in the castle," Freddie said. "I think he's dead."

"How do you know?"

"He won't eat. We gave him fish food. You can see it on the rocks."

"Wake up and eat," I said, tapping the glass. It was too dark to see anything in the castle. Freddie put both hands on the glass. He coughed, staring into the glass with his mouth open. I could hear a rattle in his chest as he breathed.

"Wake up," I said, tapping the glass.

"He's dead," Freddie said.

Antonio drove me back to my mother's house, and I stood in the yard and watched him drive away. It was dark and I wanted to go for a walk. The air was cold and the sky seemed to open up with a midnight blue. I walked down Fulton Road, past the neighboring houses with slanted roofs and smoke billowing from chimneys. Telephone wires intersected in the dark sky. I walked down winding roads, past dark tree shapes in the yellow light of the streetlamps. Moonlight reflected on the damp street. My breath was a constant plume of smoke in the chilly air. Soon fatigue came over me and I had the brief sensation I was falling. I stood in the middle of the road in the night and welcomed the silence. In the distance I saw the old White Antelope Inn, which was vacant now. The White Antelope Inn had chandeliers made of elk horns, an old jukebox and windows covered with heavy velvet drapes. A Hungarian gypsy band played on Saturday nights during the summer months. The 77-year-old owner, a smalltime bookie and friend of Gene's, was forced to close the place down at some point due to illegal gambling in the back room after hours.

I stood in the middle of the road in the moonlight. I needed sleep. As I walked back I checked my phone: still no message from Meg.

18

I dreamt about being lost in a crowded train station again. The train station was never the same place, but always crowded. I was walking through a crowd, trying to find someone. I stepped out on a platform and heard the roar of a train passing on the tracks. Everybody around me was in a hurry. I saw myself standing across the room, looking around.

The noise of a train woke me and I rolled over on my back. I was alone in the dark. I noticed it was four in the morning and I couldn't get back to sleep.

In the morning I raked mulch in the flowerbeds, then climbed a ladder on the side of the house and cleaned leaves out of the gutter. When I came in Gene was walking around the house, checking the air vents, which was something he did from time to time. He was always concerned there wasn't enough air blowing out of them. I could practically smell him, feel the vigor of his presence. In the kitchen I poured a cup of coffee and spread peach jam on a bagel. Gene had made omelets, but the skillet was empty.

Soon he stepped into the kitchen and sat down at the table. "I appreciate you helping out this morning," he said in a quiet voice.

"Not a problem."

"Let's talk about what we're doing today." He was whispering to avoid waking my mother. "I was thinking we could play cards or dominoes. Chickenfoot, spades, gin rummy, something like that."

"How about chess?"

"I hate chess. It's a slow game. One game takes forever and causes brutal headaches. I'm a card player."

"I'll play chess. No cards, no dominoes. Just chess."

"Fine," he whispered. "We'll do it your way. But we should at least videotape our game so we can watch it later with your mother."

"You think she'll want to watch a videotape of us playing chess?"

"We're doing this for your mother, remember."

He got up and went into the living room, where he set up the video camera on a tripod. It was pointed at the chessboard on the card table.

"You're seriously gonna do this?" I whispered.

"Shhh. Your mother wakes up you're fucked."

"I'm whispering."

"Sit, goddamn it. Just sit and let's play."

I sat at the card table and set up my pieces. Gene hit the record button on the video camera and sat across from me. The first game was over quickly: He moved his queen out early and I put him in checkmate in six moves. Second game, five moves. Third game he played more conservatively and was able to keep his king guarded. I attacked early, wiping out a bishop and knight. Gene's face was twisted pink with frustration as he tried to move his queen. I threatened his king, ultimately stole his queen and held it high in my fist. A moment later I mated him.

"Game goddamn over," Gene whispered. He clicked off the video camera. "When your mother gets up she can watch us interact. Now we'll go outside and do something physical. It's my turn to pick a game. Let's throw the football around a little bit."

"You're not serious."

"I'm completely serious."

"But you hate football. You've always hated football."

"Horseshit. Just because I never watched doesn't mean I hated it."

I went into the kitchen and poured another cup of coffee and flipped through the newspaper. Around eleven my mother finally got out of bed. Gene had put on a sweatshirt and sneakers and a light jacket. I'd never played football, but I considered myself of average athletic ability. I played little league baseball until junior high school. I could throw and catch a football. I knew I wasn't too out of shape. Gene and I went outside in the cold with a football he'd found in the attic. I stood across from him in the yard, wearing Meg's coat, blowing on my hands to keep them warm. Gene tossed me a wobbly pass and I caught it.

"Hold on a minute," he called out. I waited while he held his shoulder and rotated it a few times. "I'm tight," he said. "The shoulder gets tight. The back, too. I need to warm up."

"Take your time," I called out. It was freezing outside and clouds of steam came out of our mouths when we talked.

"Almost ready," he said.

I took off Meg's coat and dropped it in the yard while he kept rotating his shoulder. For a moment I didn't care about freezing. I threw a hard spiral too low and he tried to catch it, nearly falling as he went after it. He picked up the ball and took a moment for himself, looking at it, feeling it with his hands. The wind was out of the north, too cold for this. Did it seem crazy, two men out here playing catch with a football? Gene took a step and threw the ball back to me, another wobbly pass.

I threw another low spiral, out of his reach. The ball landed in front of him and bounced away.

"You throw terrible," he said. "No wonder you couldn't play sports."

This went on for about ten minutes. I kept waiting for him to tell me he'd had enough, but he toughed it out. I was getting pissed off and we were both freezing.

I threw it over his head, causing him to lift his arms and grasp air. I threw it hard to his left, out of his reach.

"Terrible," he called out. "You throw like a damn fool."

I turned and threw it over the fence to the backyard, which really made him mad.

"You dumbshit, what are you doing?"

I'd had enough. I charged at him. He had time to get ready, so I went low, diving into his legs. I felt him tumble over me and yell out in pain. When I got up, I saw he was lying on his back, moaning.

"You broke it," he said. "You little shit. I can't move."

"Yeah right."

"My fucking back," he said. He wasn't moving. He lay there breathing heavily. I knelt down on one knee to help him, but that's when he grabbed my arm and pulled me to the ground. He rolled over and twisted my arm behind my back and pressed my face down into the cold grass. I could feel his weight pressing down on me.

I yelled for him to stop.

"Was that an apology?"

"Get off me," I said.

He let go of my arm and released pressure from my back. I turned my head and saw him reach down with a hand, offering to help me up, but I didn't budge.

"Get the fuck away from me."

He turned and walked toward the house. I could see my mother standing at the window, watching.

Later I sat in a chair in the back room, staring outside at the dim sunlight. In a movie my mother would've walked in and sat next to me. We would be showered in the last light of the day, having a mother-son talk. There would be music. The setting sun. An embrace. She would've told me how proud she was of me, how hard I tried, and that she loved me. But things never happen that way. I took out my phone, texted Basille and asked if he could come pick me up in the morning. I thought about my past, neighbors who were no longer around. Men like Mr. Koenig, a retired astronomy teacher who used to live down the road. And Pastor Wariner, who played golf on Mondays and Saturdays and taught Basille and me how to hit a golf ball in the field behind his house. I sat thinking about these men, and how different they were from Gene. It was getting dark out. Nobody bothered me for a long time while I sat staring at shadows and trees. There was nothing left for me to do to make my mother happy. I got up and walked through the living room to where Gene was sitting in a recliner watching some sort of reality TV program in which a couple was driving through a city in a big hurry to reach their destination, shouting at each other, the husband holding up a map and yelling at his wife to turn left before they were in last place and out of money. It was all about the money, the frantic driving, the screaming, the sweating.

I went into my mother's bedroom where she was sitting with her head propped up on pillows, a book in her hands. There was a glass on the nightstand beside her, a vodka cranberry. But I was glad to see her reading at least, doing something besides just lying there wallowing in her own self-pity. She looked up at me as I entered.

"I had a strange dream," she said. "I fell asleep for a minute and then woke. I was dreaming about the town I lived in when I was a little girl. I'm always dreaming of that town, the streets, our old house. I watched someone climb the water tower downtown, a man I didn't know, a street worker or something. He was climbing to jump to his death, or at least that's what I kept thinking in my dream. I was standing across the street from the water tower, watching him climb. He saw me and waved. He was about to commit suicide. I thought about that in my dream."

"Did he jump?"

"I woke up before. My dreams are always like that, watching things happen to other people instead of doing things. I'm a born watcher, I think."

"I was thinking about heading back to Dallas tomorrow."

"Oh," she said. "Gene can drive you."

"Basille said he's coming over tomorrow. I'll catch a ride back to Meg's with him. You seem to be feeling better. That makes me feel better."

"Good," she said.

She arched her back. She was powerless to pain and her own immobility. For too long she'd remained in bed, alone, plotting the winter weather and her own silence. We could've gathered around her bed, praising her or begging her; it didn't matter. I understood that she would come out of her depression when she chose to, and nothing I could say would change that.

The next afternoon Basille came over. Gene and I still weren't talking. Neither of us had apologized. I'd already done laundry and packed my bag in my old bedroom. Basille arrived in time for lunch. We were all sitting in the living room when he came in. Our mother and Gene were eating on trays in front of the TV. Gene had made omelets.

Basille collapsed onto the couch and mumbled something about not being in a good mood. Gene shushed us, turning up the volume on the TV with the remote. He and our mother were engrossed, as usual, in the news. The news anchor said: "In Joplin,

Missouri, doctors say that an infant born with flipper arms smiled for the first time."

Basille went into the kitchen and made himself an omelet. He stood eating in the room. I had déjà vu watching Basille standing there taking a bite of omelet and chewing with his mouth open while we all sat in the living room. The local news anchor was talking to a woman who was a lobbyist for an environmental group. They were in downtown Fort Worth.

"I'm feeling weird today," Basille said. "For no reason."

Gene pointed the remote at the TV and read the digital guide on the screen: "Classic sitcom outtakes on channel eighty-three tonight," he said. "Some of the funniest outtakes from classic sitcoms such as *Three's Company, The Bob Newhart Show, Happy Days* and *All in the Family*."

"I feel numb," Basille said.

Our mother was staring at the TV while Gene scrolled through the digital guide. Basille finished eating and flipped through the newspaper, reading aloud his horoscope. Soon we were ready to go.

"Make sure to keep your phone on in case I need you," Gene said to him. He looked at me. "You too."

I knew what he meant. He wanted to talk about Meg and then go see Axel. I slung my bag over my shoulder and thanked them. Gene didn't get up. He gave a slight wave with his hand, staring at the TV. Our mother walked us to the door. She told us to drive safe and walked back into the living room.

19

On the drive back to Deep Ellum I asked Basille if he had talked to Meg. "I didn't want to say anything back there in front of Mom and Gene," I said.

"I texted her about going out to Red Owl with me but she didn't text back."

"Something's weird."

"I think you're right," he said.

Basille needed to ride the bus when he felt anxious. When we got back to Dallas we went from bus to bus, riding around the city. I didn't mind going with him. I read the *Dallas Morning News* that someone had left in the seat.

"No hug goodbye," he said. "Did she hug you once while you were there?"

"No."

"I can tell she's doing better. She's out of bed. She's watching TV." He leaned his head against the window and stared at the world passing by. I offered him a Hydrocodone but he declined, which was good because I was getting low.

Once, when he was young and still grieving over the National Geography Bee debacle, Basille was suspended from school for a week for taking Gene's pistol and pointing it at his head. This happened on a spring day when he met with Mrs. Wills, the principal, about an issue he was having in the classroom, over an argument with a teacher about a grade. The teacher wasn't present, but Mrs. Wills sided with the teacher, and in retaliation Basille reached into his backpack and retrieved the gun and pointed it at his head, stating that if Mrs. Wills wouldn't call the teacher into her office at that moment that he would shoot himself in the head right in front of her. Mrs. Wills called security instead of the teacher. Basille willfully handed over the gun. He wasn't going to shoot himself, he said. He wasn't going to hurt anyone.

He was suspended and sent to counseling for several months. He never talked about it, and nobody in the family ever brought it up.

"I keep dreaming I'm back in school," Basille said now, leaning his head against the bus's foggy window. "Except I'm an adult. I walk through hallways, trying to find my class, worried about not graduating. I'm carrying my trumpet, looking for the band room. I walk around aimlessly and everything looks and feels the same as it did when I was in school. Is that a common dream?"

"I think so."

"We've both lost weight, I think. What's the deal? I can't eat around certain kids. Certain kids turn my stomach the same way redheads do. Is that weird?"

"A little."

"It's like eating eggs. I can only eat eggs when people aren't watching or paying attention. If someone's watching me, forget it. The same way with drinking milk. I can't look at certain people or let anyone watch me."

"Strange."

"I need a dog," Basille said. "A black lab or collie mix, something big that I can take on walks in the park. The more I have to scoop up its shit and place it in a little baggy the better. You have to embrace these things I guess."

We got off the bus and then sat and waited for another. There was an old homeless woman sitting beside us who was talking to herself.

"The other day I was walking in the park and I saw a pile of shit," Basille said. "Just sitting there in the grass. The grass around it was dead. It wasn't dog shit. It was just sitting there in a pile. I wondered how many people had walked by and seen this same pile of human shit. Did it bother them? All day it kept popping in my mind."

"Likely a large dog," I said.

Another bus arrived and we got on. We found a seat near the back.

"Since when did you get so bothered by shit?" I asked.

"I was on a date last year with a girl I liked and who really liked me. We went out to dinner and then went back to her place and were just hanging out. You know, just watching TV and talking. Then all of a sudden she went to the bathroom in the hall and closed the door. I heard the extra little click so I knew she locked it. She was in there a good eight or nine minutes. I finally heard the toilet flush and then the hiss of air-freshener. I was certain she sprayed Lysol. The door opened and she returned to the couch, and I was fucking amazed that she'd just taken a dump and it didn't bother her on such an early date."

I changed the subject and told him that Gene wanted to pay a visit to Axel to confront him about Meg.

"Yeah, yeah," he said. "That sounds like a good idea."

I met Desi at a place called Sophabella's when she got off work. She ordered a glass of wine and I drank a Racer 5 IPA. She was wearing a hair clip that held her bangs back and I could really see her whole face. I told her I liked her skin.

"The winter makes it dry," she said. "But thanks. What are you doing for the rest of the day?"

"Nothing," I said. "I don't have to go back to work until tomorrow. What about you?"

She was doing something with her phone.

"Let's go after this drink," she said.

We went back to her apartment. I stopped in upstairs to see if Meg was there but the place was empty. We drank wine and listened to music at Desi's. I heard voices outside the door of people returning home from work. Soon it was dark and we were drunk and in her bedroom. Desi got on top of me and licked my neck and ear. I took off her shirt and watched her unfasten her bra and free her breasts. We were soon tangled in her covers.

"What do you want me to do?" she asked.

"Nothing."

"You can do whatever you want."

I told her I didn't want to do anything. She sat up in bed and I hugged her waist. I told her I wanted to go to sleep with her.

"What's wrong?" she said.

"Nothing. I just like this."

We lay there quiet for a while. Then she got out of bed and put her shirt on and then went into the bathroom. When she came out she stood staring at me.

"I don't understand you," she said.

She waited for me to say something. I said, "I just want to be here with you. That's all." I sat up and looked out the window. "Do you want me to go?"

"Maybe," she said.

I got out of bed and walked out without saying anything and went upstairs to Meg's. I tried to grasp the gravity of what had just happened. Meg was gone somewhere and I was still sort of drunk. In the kitchen I filled a glass of water then went over by the window and turned on the turntable. I put on one of Meg's jazz records, something by Chet Baker. I sat in the chair and smoked. I kept thinking Desi would come upstairs and knock on the door. Or that Meg would text me. I texted Sawyer: *What's up? If you're not doing anything, come over to Meg's and let's hang out.* For a couple of hours I just listened to music and tried not to think about anything else.

20

Sawyer showed up late. He was wearing a hooded sweatshirt and gloves and old jeans. "You ever answer your phone?" he asked.

"Not really."

"I quit my job at Taco Hut. I told my boss, Jim, to go fuck himself. He wanted me to mop up vomit and shit in the bathroom. I couldn't do it."

He sat down on the couch and ran a hand over his face. Then he went into a long monologue about some reoccurring fantasy he had, where he was a special agent having an affair with his boss's wife.

I stared out the window while he talked. It was dark and empty outside.

"... she likes me to talk to her while we fuck," he was saying. "Wants me to tell her I'm younger and stronger than her husband and that I take digestive enzymes and antioxidants and potent biotic soft gels. The fantasy recurs every couple of months or so."

By now I was sober. We split a frozen burrito that I microwaved, then Sawyer headed out. I walked with him downstairs. I saw a woman in the hall who was taking out the garbage, carrying two large trash sacks. She walked with a limp and was having trouble so I offered to help.

We walked outside to the dumpster along the side of the building. She was a small woman with frazzled hair, probably in her fifties. She wore an old T-shirt, ripped a little in the neck. She looked exhausted.

"You live upstairs, right?" she asked.

"With my sister."

We walked back into the building and she checked her mailbox while she continued to talk. "Sorry if my son is too loud," she said.

"He's trying to build a birdhouse for school, so maybe you heard him hammering. His name is George."

"I haven't heard anything," I said.

"My husband left us two years ago. He was a welder. You want coffee or something? It's freezing out."

I got the sense she was lonely and I felt sorry for her. She lived next door to Desi. As we passed Desi's door I heard music coming from inside her apartment.

The woman introduced herself as Alice. Her apartment was small and dark and smelled of onions. Her son was sitting on the couch watching a small TV. He held a tube in his mouth that connected to a small black box that buzzed.

"That's George," she said. "He has asthma. I have to give him these breathing treatments twice a day."

I saw a hammer and pieces of wood painted white on the floor next to the window. George was about nine or ten. He didn't look over at us or acknowledge my presence. He sat on the couch, staring at the TV, breathing in and out with the tube in his mouth.

Alice made us coffee and invited me to sit with them and watch TV. She sat next to George and helped him with his tube. I sat in a chair and watched as she held the tube for him while he sat there, staring at the TV. His chest was rising and falling. Mucus gathered around his nose and upper lip.

"George likes birds," she told me. "His art teacher is letting him build a birdhouse. The other kids in his class aren't able to do much. It's a special school, the one just north of here. I was thinking about pulling George out of there, though. One of their teachers was arrested last month for killing his dog. Maybe you saw it on the news."

"I didn't."

"This guy beat his dog to death with a crow bar. A Doberman, big dog. It apparently bit him so he beat it with the crow bar until it died. He made his stepson help him clean up the blood off the floor and carry the dog to the truck to take to the dump. The kid told his mom what happened and they arrested the guy at the school the next day. What is it with people these days?"

She tapped the breathing tube with a finger and then turned off the black box. George wiped his nose with the heel of his hand

and sniffed. An old cowboy movie was on TV. Alice put her arm around her son and brought his head to her shoulder. George continued to stare at the TV with his mouth open.

"A man tried to break into our apartment once," she said. "This was when my husband Frank was still here. Frank nearly beat that man to death."

"Was he armed?"

"He didn't have shit. Some dumbass, huh? Who breaks into an apartment without a weapon? The guy was high on meth or coke or something. All bug-eyed. Said he thought he had the wrong apartment. My husband beat his ass real good. Had him down on the floor right there where you're sitting. Then he called the police and they came and arrested the man."

"Jesus."

"George was a baby. That was right before Frank left. He left us in December, just before Christmas. That was a rough year. It was a hard Christmas. What do you do when your husband leaves for good and you still have to think about Christmas? You drink, that's what you do. That's what I did. I was messed up for a while. If it wasn't for George I would've drank myself straight to hell. I'm eight years sober this coming March. I thank the good Lord Jesus Christ for helping me through it. Do you know Jesus personally?"

"I don't know," I said.

I excused myself and went into the bathroom. I put my hands on the sink and looked at myself in the mirror. I touched my face, examining the odd parts. My face was unshaven and pale.

When I came out I thanked Alice for the coffee and told her I needed to go. She was next to George with her eyes closed, whispering. Maybe she was praying. George was sitting with his head leaning against her shoulder. I could hear the wheeze in his asthmatic breathing.

I left the building and started walking down Crowdus. I passed a man in a stocking cap who was scraping his windshield. He was leaning over the hood, really scraping hard. There was something sad and fatherly about him. He was an older man with glasses, wearing a heavy coat and scarf. An attorney probably, or an accountant with a large firm in midtown Dallas. A man who lived in a suburb but stopped by here to visit his son. A man who paid for his son's college tuition and allowed him to pursue the dream of painting, or avant-garde filmmaking, or being a novelist. A man who will return home to his wife of thirty-seven years. He'll remove his coat and hang it up in the hall closet. He'll sit across from his wife at the dinner table and the two will eat in silence, head down. Then he'll help his wife put up dishes after dinner and take off his shoes and sit in a recliner so that he can read the newspaper by the light of the lamp.

For a moment I considered stopping to help but then reconsidered and kept walking south. I thought I would walk over to the liquor store and buy a six-pack of beer when my phone beeped. I expected it to be Meg, but it was Puig. The text said: *Gideon, I'm a mess. Earlier I got a threatening letter. Sophia and I got into a fight and I kicked her out. Need to talk. Can u give me a call or stop by?*

So I skipped the liquor store and instead headed toward Puig's building. When I arrived it was worse than I had expected. He was limping and walking with a cane from falling on the ice a few days earlier. He told me he was lonely and sad, hadn't left his apartment in three days. He poured us a brandy in the kitchen.

"Thanks for coming. I'm a mess tonight."

"Not a problem," I said.

He had a reddish wine stain on his collar. His shirt was unbuttoned and untucked. He'd been drinking but wasn't completely drunk. He handed me a glass of brandy and sat in the armchair across from me.

"I'm getting anonymous letters," he said. "Someone hates me. It's because of Sophia. She's half my age and someone doesn't like that."

"Who?"

"Could be anyone. A former lover. An ex-boyfriend. She denied everything, but I think she knows who it is. I caught her whispering on her cell phone in the bathroom. Sneaking off in the middle of the night to see a woman I later found out was a former lover of hers. And now someone is sending me typewritten letters, watching me through binoculars from the roof of a building across the street."

"Watching you?"

"Someone's following me," he said. "It started a few days ago. That's when I slipped on the ice and hurt my back. I was carrying a sack of groceries from the market and as I walked out I noticed the guy who held the door for me was wearing dark glasses and looking down. He followed me all the way from Third Street. I turned down an alley and he was there. I'd turn around and he was there." He set his glass down on a table of varnished black wood. "Sophia was in exploitation films," he said. "I think maybe it's those people. There are things I can't go into."

Poor old Puig. I felt compelled to listen and make sense of what he was saying. He spoke of Sophia's life like a father missing a child. He spoke of her small hands and the way she covered her eyes when she was upset or embarrassed. These people were dangerous and now he believed they were after him. And yet, despite my sympathy for him, I still found myself—even after the brandy he gave me—feeling apprehensive and worried about Meg.

"You're distracted by something," he said. "I can tell. You're an easy read, Gideon—anyone ever tell you that?"

"I know, I know," I said.

He offered me another drink and I obliged. He wanted to know about my past girlfriends. We talked about loneliness and fear and sadness and the need to feel loved. He started getting drunk.

"Can I share something with you?" he asked. "It's really personal." He saw that I didn't mind. "When I was younger I was burned. It's a long story. The specifics aren't important here, the point is that I had to learn to forgive. I had to learn to like my body all over again. It's just one area, right here on my lower stomach and groin. For years I was ashamed of my body and avoided any real sexual contact with anyone. It took until my late thirties before it didn't bother me."

He paused, as if waiting for a response. I didn't say anything. I nodded and he continued.

"I did some weird shit in the seventies and early eighties," he said. "I was younger then. Anyway, none of that matters. I've gotten used to my skin and the area where I was burned. I don't mind sharing this with people, you have to understand. I'm not deformed." He told me he felt close enough to me to share this, said he wasn't ashamed of himself. He was unbuttoning his pants, bleary-eyed, drunk. He lifted his shirt and told me not to be shocked. Then he exposed himself.

There was burned flesh. A putrescence of clotted skin. Mutilation. The gelatinous area of burned skin was stretched and discolored. A disfigurement. It took what felt like a long time for the horror to diminish, and I felt the gravity of the moment closing in. I found myself standing and heading for the door.

"Wait," he said. "Gideon, it's not what you think." He buttoned his pants and came toward me, but I told him I needed to leave before Meg came home. He kept saying, "It's not what you think." I hurried out and heard him calling after me as I reached the bottom of the stairs and left the building.

21

When I got back to the apartment Meg was there. I hadn't seen her in several days. She was sitting on the floor, doing something with a photo album. She looked up at me when I came in.

"You're here," I said. I looked toward the bedroom, thinking maybe someone else was there, but she told me we were alone.

"I was thinking about going to see Mom," she said. "How is she?"

I sat on the floor across from her. I took one of her Marlboro Lights from her pack on the floor and lit it. "She kept asking about you," I said. "I think she just wants to see you."

"She wants to worry about me all the time," she said. "She wants to tell me how to live my life."

I could see the frustration and sadness in her face. Maybe there were some things I didn't know that had happened between them.

"I think she's just sad," I said.

Meg flipped through pages in the album. "Hey, remember this?" There were photographs of us at her birthday party when she turned nine. We were at a place called White Rabbit's, a kid-friendly, *Alice in Wonderland*-themed restaurant located in an old warehouse in downtown Dallas. I'd forgotten all about it. Meg had an obsession with the place. When you walked in, a server introduced you to the White Rabbit, who was a person dressed in a full white bunny suit who didn't speak. A winding staircase leading down to the main dining room was decorated with all kinds of fake shrubbery and tall grass, which was supposed to mimic the experience of going down the rabbit hole. I remember walking down that staircase to the main dining room, a dim and sort of spooky room with tall ceilings and dark walls. There were tables with tablecloths of all different colors—purple and pink and yellow and red—and characters from *Alice in Wonderland* walked around and talked to kids. The place shut down after surviving less than two years because one of the employees, a teenage boy, threw a candy apple and hit a young girl in the mouth, busting her lip open. This resulted in what turned out to be an ugly lawsuit against the restaurant's owner and mastermind, none other than Axel Mangus, who at the time was in his mid-thirties. After this, and a few other failed ventures including a proposed Hollywood theme park, Axel apparently had a nervous breakdown. Axel was admitted to the psychiatric ward at St. Francis Hospital for trying to set himself on fire in a failed suicide attempt.

Meg showed me an article from *The Dallas Arts*, saying that Axel Mangus "was no longer the man businessmen and former patrons of White Rabbit's knew him to be." According to the article, Axel claimed he wasn't trying to commit suicide but that he'd had a drug habit for several years and that he'd been recently contacted by HBO to be one of the subjects of a documentary on crack-cocaine addiction in the business world.

"So this is the Axel I keep hearing about," I said.

Meg looked confused.

"People keep saying you're with some guy Axel," I said. "Is this your dealer? Are you seeing him?"

"It's not like that," she said. "Not anymore. He was my dealer for a while. I was seeing him, sort of. We were hanging out some when I was going through that breakup with A.J.—you remember him? He took me out and treated me well."

She went into the bathroom and turned on the bathwater. A moment later I pulled off my shoes and went in there and got into the tub with my clothes on. She let me wash her hair. I put my hands in the bathwater and leaned back and closed my eyes. We heard someone upstairs walking around. A dog barked from somewhere outside. We heard a train from the track nearby.

Eventually I got out of the tub and undressed. Then got into her bed, under the covers. I was cold. When she got into bed I was turned away from her, watching frost gather on the window. Outside, the world was illuminated with distant lightning, the thunder of sleet and snow showers. I turned and lay on my back. Meg gazed at me as I stared at the shadows moving on the ceiling.

Somewhere on the street outside a garbage truck rumbled and then drove away with a clatter.

"I should tell you," she said. "He hit me once. Axel. It was a while ago, you don't need to worry. Just don't mention it to Gene. Everything's fine now."

I didn't say anything, but I felt a rush of anger. Meg turned and put her arms around me. We were like kids. Even though in this moment she was open and affectionate toward me, I doubted she would be the same in the morning.

I went to work the next day. Vince had me restring guitars in back and inventory merchandise throughout the store. I didn't mind the work. Rick and Vince dealt with the customers and gave guitar lessons to young kids. At the end of the day I vacuumed the whole store and used a box knife to cut the packing tape from boxes so I could fold them up and haul them to the dumpster out back.

For a week I didn't see Meg. She came home during the day when I was at work. After work I usually bought a six-pack of beer and went straight back to her apartment and watched TV all night. I told myself I wasn't going to text her but after a few days I was starting to feel lonely. I wanted to go back to Chicago, where I felt I belonged. In Dallas all I was doing was walking around, brooding. There was more in Chicago for me, even if I didn't know what it was.

As I was walking back to the apartment one evening with a six-pack in a paper sack, I saw Meg leaving the building. She didn't see me. Instead of going to her car she started walking south. I crossed the street and followed her, down Crowdus and over to Malcolm X. She turned and disappeared around the side of the next building. I hurried to the end of the building to peek around the corner. She continued south. There was a fenced playground in the area between us. I walked along the side of the fence as she headed toward another building. Straight ahead I saw parked cars in a small lot. Someone, a man, was ahead of her, hurrying into the building where Meg was headed. The man climbed the steps leading to a back door of the building. Meg followed him, climbing the steps and entering through the same door.

A couple of teenage boys were playing basketball in the playground. They didn't notice me as I walked past them toward the building. I approached the building and stopped at the stairs. I expected the door to be locked, but it wasn't—it opened to a long, dim hallway with doors on both sides. The hallway was warm, well kept. The floor was old carpet. Someone walked toward me, stopping to light a cigarette—an older man, wearing a denim shirt and old jeans and work boots. He asked if I needed some help.

"I was looking for someone," I said. "I thought she might be here."

The man noticed the bottles of beer in my bag. "A.A. meets here, buddy. Looks like you're in the wrong place."

"OK," I said. "Sorry."

The man stepped past me and went outside. I stood in the hallway for a moment. Meg would've told me if she was going to A.A. meetings. In truth, I didn't know what to think. Maybe she was meeting a friend. Being a support. But I knew Meg wasn't much of a support in staying away from drugs and alcohol. I left and walked back to the apartment.

When I got back I'd just put the beer in the fridge when I heard a knock on the door. It was Desi. She stood there in the hallway, looking at me, a slight figure with a drawn face, her hair pulled back in a ponytail. She waited for me to invite her in. I held the door for her and returned to the kitchen for a beer.

"I thought we should talk," she said. She took one of my cigarettes from the coffee table and lit it. She sat down on the couch and looked up at me. I stood across from her.

"For the past few days I've been in a weird funk," she said. "I'm sorry about the other night."

"It's OK."

"I don't know what I was thinking. I was sort of drunk and I like you."

I wasn't sure what to say to her, so I apologized too.

"Are you doing anything tonight?" she asked. "I mean, if not, I have discount passes to the ice skating rink. Do you skate?"

"Not in a long time. I'm really not very good."

"Oh, come on."

"I'll go, but I'm not good."

I put on Meg's coat and Desi drove us to the rink near downtown. I had trouble pulling on my skates and tying the laces. I'd only ice-skated a couple of times in my life.

"You'll do great," she said.

When we got out on the ice, she took my hand and helped me. I was able to skate beside her, slowly, until we came to the turn. I tried to step with my right foot but lost my balance and fell, bringing Desi down with me. We were both laughing. She managed to help me up and I held the rail for balance.

"You really are terrible," she said. We were still laughing.

Afterwards, when we walked to her car, she took my hand and held it. We got in her car and I leaned over and kissed her. We sat in her car for a while and talked.

"My mom's going out to dinner with me tomorrow night," she said. "We're pretty close. When I was little one time she told me how mice were used in genetic experiments to aid in scientific studies. She bought me a children's encyclopedia set and went through it with me whenever I asked questions, but mostly I just looked at the illustrations and pictures: Michelangelo's statue of David, ancient tombs, constellations."

"I'm not sure where you're going with this."

"I'm just telling you about my parents," she said. She wanted to open up and I let her. "My dad would be in one place and then instantly in another. When I read in bed at night he'd come in to tell me to turn the lamp off, and then I'd look up and he'd be gone. He volunteered to help coach my second grade soccer league one year. I quit after the first game when he didn't show. Something came up, was his excuse. There weren't many things he liked to do except go hunting. Sometimes I watched him clean his shotgun or feed the baby quail he kept in a big pen in the backyard. He would let me hold them. They were so small, their little heads jerking, too little to fly. I considered them pets and told my class all about them, how they hopped around in their pen and that someday I would train them to fly around in my bedroom and bring me my dresses, just like in *Cinderella*. But it wasn't like that at all. My dad raised them with the intent of later setting them free to hunt. He drank coffee from a thermos on cold winter mornings before he went hunting. I'd wake up and look out my window to see him carrying his shotgun to his pickup. He wore camouflage hunting clothes and a hat."

She looked at me, waiting for me to say something.

"So did you ever go hunting with him?" I asked.

"Once. I had a great time. Is that weird? I don't look the type. What about your family?"

"You don't want to hear about it."

"I do."

I told her about my real dad dying when I was young and how my mother struggled to raise me and Meg and Basille on her own until Gene came along. I didn't go into specifics. I didn't want to talk about anything really.

When we got back to the apartment building she said she had to be up early to meet her mother for breakfast. "I should probably go to bed," she said. "I had a good time tonight. Thanks."

I told her I had a good time too when we reached her door, knowing we were not going in her apartment together. Somehow I didn't mind. Nor did I mind that we hugged in front of her door before she went inside. Then I went upstairs to Meg's apartment, hung up Meg's coat and stared for a minute at the frost on the window, trying to imagine Desi with a shotgun, hunting with her father.

22

A couple of days went by with no word from Meg. I was beginning to worry. Every time I texted her she would text back telling me she was OK and not to worry. Gene was worried too. He called me as I was flipping through the channels on TV. On the national news a weatherman was live in Buffalo, talking about record amounts of snow. There seemed to be snow everywhere in the country. Cities were shown with snowplows in the streets. People shoveling their driveways. Trees with crystal ice hanging from branches. Schools canceled, kids sledding down hills. Cars sliding into ditches.

"There's snow everywhere," I said.

"It's bad," Gene said. "We're headed for an ice age."

"The earth is burning."

"The earth will freeze before it burns. Winters are getting worse. When do you remember a winter in Texas so fucking crazy?"

"Did you call just to talk about the weather?"

"I made some calls about Axel," he said. "Did some research through my friend Jane, the journalist. Axel's living in an apartment above an old deserted movie theatre downtown called The Riviera. The city just bought the building. They're getting ready to gut the place and do a whole renovation."

"The Riviera," I said. "Yeah, I know the place."

"He's holed up in some crappy infested shithole with Meg. I can just picture it. Meg in there with that sorry asshole."

"I'm going over there," I said.

"Not without me you're not."

I knew not to argue with him, so I told him we'd do it later. Though I'm sure he knew I was lying.

"Don't go alone," he said. "Do not."

After we hung up I took my last Hydrocodone and sat in a

chair in front of the window. Soon I could hear noises from the apartment above, footsteps, someone pacing.

Sometime late in the night Puig knocked on the door. I was half asleep when I answered, drowsy from the pill. I didn't mind seeing him. I let him in and right away he apologized for barging in so late.

"No problem. Really."

"I should've considered your feelings. I can't help it sometimes."

"It's really OK."

He sat across from me and lit a cigarette. "You remind me of me when I was younger. Maybe that's why I feel I can open up to you. I hope your mother's doing OK?"

"Better I think."

"My father suffered from severe depression like your mother, which made my own mother furious. My mother saw my father's depression as a crutch to the family. It was beginning to affect my brother. 'Look at him,' my mother told him. 'Look at my son, sitting at the table all by himself, sulking. Not eating. Just sitting there. This is your fault.' My poor father. It affected my behavior at school. It caused severe anxiety for me."

The lamp beside him was on. He sat forward and stared at me in a cloud of blue smoke.

"I liked to masturbate at school," he said. "Whenever I got a chance, during class, I asked to go to the bathroom and closed the stall door. I'd read bathroom graffiti, words like *cock* and *pussy* and *tits*. With a knife I'd carve my initials into the stall door and feel a tinge of excitement. I thought of teachers. It was all a sort of escape. My way of dealing with the anxiety. I got it from my father. He vomited anytime he and my mother got into an argument ..."

I fell asleep for a moment, and when I opened my eyes Puig was still sitting forward, talking in a firm voice:

"... when he came home from work, he came in through the front door, removed his jacket and set his briefcase down on the coffee table. The first thing he did was go to the bathroom, then return to the living room and read the newspaper in his recliner until dinner was ready. After dinner, he changed into a bathrobe and slippers and watched the evening news. The rest of the evening he opened his briefcase and marked papers with a red pen. My earliest memories involved my parents sitting in silence for hours at a time: my father in his recliner, my mother in her chair across the room, reading or knitting socks. My brother spent much of his time alone in his bedroom, playing with army figures or talking to himself or smashing things. Sometimes my mother sat him on her lap and read to him, but there wasn't a lot of family time spent together. I can't remember a time when we had any sort of family conversation at home."

I stood up, trying to stay awake. Puig suggested we go for coffee down the street. I put on Meg's coat and walked with him in the cold, to prolong the night a little longer.

★

I slept for a few hours. Then late in the night my cell phone rang. It was Basille. He said he needed to go to the emergency room. "I'm having a heart attack or stroke or something. There's a pain in my arm and my heart is beating fast and I can't breathe."

"You're not having a heart attack," I said. "Where are you? Did you do coke or something?"

"I did, but that's not it. Something's definitely wrong, Gideon. My arm is killing me and I can't fucking breathe."

"I don't have a car. Meg's not here."

"I just need you to go with me," he said. "I'll drive over and pick you up."

"Basille, you're fine. Come over if you want, but I'm sure you're fine."

"Walking to the car now. I'm on my way."

By the time he arrived he hadn't calmed down. He stood in the doorway almost in tears. He handed me his keys and said I needed to drive.

"Look at my hands," he said. His fingers were crooked and constricted like he was making two claws. "They're tingly and numb."

"Settle down," I said. I put on Meg's coat and we left. I drove his car out to the hospital just south of downtown. Basille kept looking at his hands and asking me what was happening.

"Move your fingers," I said. "Can you move them? Do they hurt?"

"They feel numb," he said.

I dropped him off at the emergency room entrance so he could check in while I parked the car. When I got inside they'd already taken him to a small room. The woman working the desk looked tired and there were only a few people in the waiting area. She told me the room was down the hall. When I got in there, a doctor was putting an IV in Basille's arm.

"I feel better," Basille said.

"What happened?" I asked.

"He was hyperventilating," the doctor said. "It constricts the muscles in your hands. He might also be a bit dehydrated so I'm putting him on an IV for fluids."

"Hyperventilating," I said. "Why?"

"Do you take anything for panic attacks or anxiety?" the doctor asked Basille.

"Xanax," he said. "I was on Paxil for a while and before that they put me on Zoloft, but that was a long time ago."

The doctor looked at him. "No other drugs? Your heart rate was high."

"I was playing basketball with friends at the gym." Basille glanced at me. "That's about it."

The doctor wrote something down on the clipboard and said he'd be back in a bit to check on him.

"Did he want me to say I've been doing crank or something?" Basille asked me after the doctor left the room.

"Probably. I don't know. Let me see your hands."

He showed me, moving his fingers. "They're back to normal," he said. "It's like the minute he said the word 'hyperventilating' I felt better. Thanks for driving me here."

It was nearly five in the morning and I had to be up early for work. "You need to quit doing goddamn crank," I said. "That's cheap shit. You're already wired enough."

On the drive back, Basille felt well enough to smoke a cigarette. "Gene called me and told me Mom's started helping out on a ranch or something."

"A ranch?"

"Some sort of horse therapy. At least she's out of the house. She always liked horses."

"He didn't tell me. I need to go see her again."

"Gene also told me he's been looking for Meg. Said something about calling you."

"He called me. He said he found out that Axel's living in the old Riviera Theatre, and we think Meg's been staying there with him."

"You think she's dealing?"

"I don't know. I don't think so. Don't tell her I told you this, but she told me he hit her once."

Basille went quiet—I wasn't sure if he was mad or in shock. I could tell he was staring at me, but I kept my eyes on the road.

"He hit her? Why didn't you tell me this?"

"I don't know. I was half asleep when she told me."

"Motherfucker," he said.

"I know, I know."

When we got back to Meg's apartment I asked Basille if he wanted to stay but he had to get home. I went upstairs and tried to sleep. It was six in the morning and I had to be at work at nine.

23

The day dragged on. I kept my mouth shut and did my job. I had to build myself up to go see Axel Mangus. After work I took the bus downtown and went to the Riviera Theatre, which was deserted, with boarded-up windows. It was almost dark when I got there. The words "For Sale" were written in black letters on the half-collapsed marquee. I stood in front of the side doors a moment, looking at my cell phone, waiting until there were no cars or anyone around. Then I opened the glass door and stood before a staircase. There were mailboxes but I couldn't find one with Axel's name on it. Then I went outside and tried the front doors of the theatre but they were all locked. Graffiti was spray-painted across the boards, trash blew around in the wind. The old ticket booth window was dirty and cracked. I walked around the other side of the building and hoisted myself up on a rotted wooden fence. There was a side door that was open.

I tried to meet the moment with an outward calm. As I entered, the room was dark and cold. I realized I was in an old, small office of some sort. I saw a mop bucket in the corner, a broom and an old usher's vest hung up on a nail on the wall. I moved through the room and went through a doorway, where I found myself behind the counter of what used to be the concession stand. The glass counter was caked with dust and dirt. Under the glass there were dead bugs, old candy wrappers and dirty napkins. An old popcorn machine appeared broken and filthy with dirt. I stepped out from behind the counter and into the main lobby, where the walls were bare of what used to be Coming Attractions posters. There was a silver pole with a red velvet rope leading down a dark corridor. I followed the corridor that led into the dark theatre, but I stopped there. The theatre was pitch black, though I could see the white screen and

112

red curtain. I turned and walked back to the main lobby and found a side door with a staircase leading up.

There I heard laughter from upstairs. I knew it must've been Axel Mangus. There was a small styrofoam cup on one of the stairs with some sort of dark liquid, soda or coffee. I tiptoed up the stairs and heard the sound of laughter again. At the top of the staircase was a half-open door. I heard the noise of a TV coming from inside. I stopped at the doorway for a moment and felt a rush of panic—what was I doing? I had to remind myself of my purpose: to talk to this man about my sister. To tell him to stay away from her. To hear him out. Maybe he wasn't so bad after all. I tapped on the door and opened it. There I saw a man sitting in a chair, watching TV. He didn't look over at me as I entered.

He looked nothing like I'd imagined. I expected someone good-looking and dark, built in a sort of sleazy businessman way. Instead I found a man who looked like a farmer, wearing a cowboy hat and tinted black-rimmed glasses. As I stepped closer into the room I noticed he was eating a black licorice stick and had a notebook of yellow paper in his lap that he was scribbling on. He was engrossed in the program on TV. It was a documentary on whales, narrated by a man with a deep voice.

"Give me just one second," he said, staring at the TV. He sat with his notepad in his lap. He scribbled something on the pad. I saw loose sheets of paper everywhere, scattered all around the room. There were sketches of whales and narwhals. There were scribblings I couldn't make out.

"I won't be long," I said.

"Hang on," he said. He scribbled something. The documentary's narrator spoke in a quiet, low voice. On TV a whale moved underwater. The camera zoomed in on the whale's eye—one single eye, dark, unblinking, staring at the camera. Axel wrote something on his paper.

He pointed the remote at the TV and turned it off. Then he turned and looked at me.

"Are you Axel Mangus?" I asked.

He leaned back in his chair and put his snakeskin boots up on the table. Took a bite of black licorice stick and chewed. "I know, I know, there are fire hazards in this building. I got a technician

113

who comes once a month." He spoke with a southern drawl. "All the wiring will be to code." He stopped talking and squinted at me. Maybe he was trying to figure out if I looked suspicious or familiar.

"I didn't come here about that."

"Well then what is it, son?" He sat up and tipped the cowboy hat back on his forehead.

"I just need to talk to you," I said.

"Talk? I hold church downstairs every Sunday, if you want talk." He blinked and looked at something in the corner of the room. I wondered if he was high on Arwal.

"I came to talk to you about Meg."

"What did you say your name was, son?"

"Gideon. I came about my sister."

 "Your sister," he said.

"Meg."

"Meg Gray's your sister?"

"Right."

He took a bite of licorice and chewed with his mouth open. I noticed one of the pearl snaps was missing on his shirt. His boots were gray and old. "Meg tell you I was here?"

"The reason I came here was to tell you to stay away from Meg."

He took a deep breath and looked at the stick of licorice in his hand while he chewed. Then he sort of fake smiled at me through black teeth and motioned with his hand for me to continue. So I did. I told him I knew Meg was coming to see him. I told him I knew Meg was dealing and using drugs and that I wanted him to stop seeing her.

"You came in here to my establishment to say this?" he said.

"I came here to tell you to stay away from her."

He looked at me and blinked. He looked in the corner of the room and then back at me, blinking. "I think you better leave, son. Nobody comes in here and talks to me this way."

"She told me you hit her," I said. My throat was dry and I couldn't swallow. "I'll leave when you tell me you'll leave her alone. That's what I came here to tell you."

"Is that so?"

"That's so."

To my surprise, he stood up and punched me in the face and I fell backward and landed on the hardwood floor. Then he leaned down and punched me in the ribs. I coughed and clutched my stomach while he stood over me.

"You don't talk that way to me," he said. "Now you need to get the hell out of my establishment."

It took me a minute or so to get up and leave the room. I thought he might hit me again but he didn't, though I wasn't able to look at him as I got to my feet. I walked down the staircase, holding my stomach and feeling like I was about to be sick. I wanted to lie down in the street. I could feel the pain begin to throb under my eye. Outside in the cold night air I turned on the sidewalk and walked south, past the post office, past the donut shop with frost on the windows, past the old brick buildings, until I reached the bus stop, where I sat and stared up into the night sky. All I could think about was how right Gene was.

24

When I got back to Meg's apartment I splashed cold water on my face and looked at my eye in the mirror. It was vaguely red and swollen. I wrapped some ice in a rag and lay down on the couch, holding the rag on my eye. I was starting to drift off when I heard a key in the door and Meg came in. I was too tired to sit up, but I turned my head and looked at her.

"Hi," she said, and then she noticed the washrag. "What's wrong?"

"What are you doing here?"

"I came home. What happened to you?"

She took off her coat and came over to me on the divan. I put the rag back on my face but she took it and looked at my eye. She touched it lightly. "You get into a fight? What happened?"

I jerked my head away and sat up.

"Who did this?" she asked. "Why are you acting like this?"

"Don't act like you don't know."

"Know what? What are you talking about?"

I looked at her. "Axel," I said. "I went to the Riviera Theatre, which I'm sure you already know."

She looked surprised, and I knew then that she didn't know. "Axel did this? He fucking hit you?" The look in her eye, as I now saw her, was like she was someone else: a vulnerable person of true compassion, holding an ambiguous concealment, but most importantly concerned and kind-hearted.

"It was my fault," I said. And then I told her I went to see Axel because I was worried about her, and that Basille and Gene and our mother were worried about her, and that I'd overheard her and our mother arguing on the phone, and that we'd heard all sorts of bad things about Axel Mangus.

She was mad and I was surprised at her reaction. She started to leave and I told her to forget about it.

"I don't care," I said. "It doesn't really hurt anyway. I'm sorry I was trying to act so goddamn protective."

"I'm not mad at you," she said, but I wasn't sure. Sometimes she was hard to read. I took a cigarette from the pack on the coffee table and lit a match. The flame wavered in the darkness.

"I need to take a walk," she said. She put on her coat and left. I didn't think she would come back, but a little while later she did. When she came in she sat down on the divan and said she would go to Red Owl with me in the morning to see our mother.

"I guess the reason you guys are so worried about me all the time is because I don't fucking communicate with anyone," she said.

"Maybe so."

"Axel's a motherfucker," she said.

We were quiet a moment. Outside, on the street below, a bus droned by.

"Basille said Mom's working with horses on a ranch."

"I'm glad she's getting out of the house. Tomorrow we'll go out there."

"I'm glad," I said. "I think she'll like that."

In the morning my head was hurting. My eye was swollen and bruised. I brushed my teeth and got dressed while Meg took a bath. I made coffee and waited for her to get ready. I knew not to call Basille this early—we'd let him sleep in.

When Meg was ready we drove over to Basille's apartment building and took the stairs up to his door. Meg had a key, so instead of knocking we let ourselves in. He was asleep on the couch, slits of sunlight streaming in from the window. I opened the blinds and called out to him to wake him. He rubbed his eyes and said something I couldn't understand. Then he recognized me.

"What the hell," he said. "What are you doing here?"

"We're going out to Mom's," I said. "Get dressed and come with us."

He sat up and squinted from the sunlight. Dust motes floated in the stream of sunlight from the window. "What the hell happened to you?"

"He'll tell you about it in the car," Meg said. "Get up."

He looked at Meg and gave a slight wave.

"You look like hell," she said. "Go shower or brush your teeth or something."

"I have sinus problems," he said. "An infection or something. I can't smell anything."

He scratched his head with both hands and yawned while we waited. His hair was sticking up everywhere. He was always slow moving in the morning.

Meg was going through his CDs. "Chet Baker," she said. "Why don't we take these? You think Mom will want to listen to them?"

Basille shrugged. Then I told him what happened. He was mad I didn't call him to go with me to the Riviera Theatre, but he got over it. On the drive to Red Owl he asked how I was going to explain all of it to Gene.

"There's no reason for him to know," I said. "I'll just say I got in a fight."

"What if he keeps on about going to see Axel?"

"Don't worry about Axel," Meg said. "I bought some nothing dope from him, but that's it. Don't worry about Gene, I'll take care of everything."

Basille kept asking me what my plans were. Was I returning to Chicago or staying? "You should stay," he said. "There's nothing up there."

"This is the only party," I said.

Basille gave me a strange look.

"Never mind," I said.

When we got to the house, Gene was in the living room playing cards with Mel Speck, a friend of his. About once a month or so they played. Mel was a retired railroad worker, now married to a woman half his age. He knew poker. He'd served time in jail in the early seventies for cheating in Binion's Horseshoe in downtown Vegas.

They were surprised to see us and the first thing Gene did was stand and look at Meg. I could tell he was shocked to see her, but he was more surprised at my eye.

"What the hell happened?" he said.

"It's nothing," I said.

"Someone hit him," Meg said.

"In a bar," added Basille.

Mel Speck laughed and said he was proud of me.

"So what are you guys doing here?" Gene said.

"Came to see Mom," Basille said. "She here?"

"She's out at Steely Ranch," he said, sitting back down. "Mel and I are playing Texas Hold 'Em if you want in."

"No money," Basille said, "but I'll take a poker tip from Mel."

"I don't know anything," Mel shrugged. Basille badgered him long enough until he gave in: "All I know is to focus on the other players' cards, not your own," Mel said.

"That's it? Tell me something I don't already know."

"Good to see you, Meg," Gene said. "You OK?"

"I'm good," she told him, and I could tell he believed her.

"Better go before you miss her," he said. "Your mother will be glad to see you."

Meg drove us out to the ranch. It was cold but the sun was out and there was no wind. We walked from the car to the barn, but our mother wasn't in there. I heard dogs barking. There was a horse with its head lowered to crop at grass. The horse raised its head and shook its mane. I reached over the fence to pet its muzzle. "Hey there," I said. "It's okay. Good boy."

Meg came over to me and rested her arms on the fence, looking around.

Then we saw her, our mother, walking toward us. "What are you guys doing here?" she called out.

"We came to see this place," Basille said.

I tried to think of what to say to her. She stood looking at us, a woman in front of her three children. Her hair was a lighter shade of gray in the sun and hung down in her eyes. I hadn't seen her outside in a long time. Even though the wind was cold, the sun was warm in a way that made me aware of sight and temperature. I hadn't seen our mother in such a light.

"What happened to your face?" she asked me. But she knew I didn't want to talk about it. She always knew. "Follow me to the barn," she said.

It seemed this would be the moment of a great communication for all of us, but as we walked along the fence toward the barn, nobody said anything. Maybe I expected Meg and our mother to just apologize to each other. As we reached the gate and our mother invited us in to follow her, Basille and I stayed behind and left her to have time alone with Meg. I don't know what they said to each other that afternoon, and in truth I don't care. Maybe we were all getting better.

Basille and I shared a cigarette and I told him I didn't have to go back to Chicago. I no longer felt alone in the world in a way that somehow gave me a strange grace. Something was changing. All around us, ice was hanging everywhere, from tree branches and fence posts, from the rooftop of the barn and from the telephone poles. All around us, ice was melting.